Sue's Secondhand Horse

BOOKS BY PHILLIP VIERECK

The Summer I Was Lost
Let Me Tell You About My Dad
The New Land
Eskimo Island
Independence Must Be Won

Sue's Secondhand

Horse

Phillip Viereck

The John Day Company · New York

An Intext *Publisher*

Library of Congress Cataloging in Publication Data

Viereck, Phillip.
    Sue's secondhand horse.

    SUMMARY: A thirteen-year-old girl's dream is realized when she receives a mare
for Christmas, an event that changes the lives of all her family in many ways.
    [1. Horses—Stories]   I. Title.
PZ7.V667St   [Fic]   72–12085
ISBN 0–381–99639–5

Second Impression, 1973

The John Day Company, 257 Park Avenue South, New York, N.Y. 10010
Published on the same day in Canada by Longman Canada Limited.

Printed in the United States of America
Designed by The Etheredges

A WORLD FAMOUS HORSE STORY Selection

Sue's Secondhand Horse

1.

Trees overhead and on both sides formed a blurring arch of green. The narrow road dipped, twisted, and climbed, all in one swaying roaring motion as Sue, her hair whipping behind her, craned her neck to peer with squinty, teary eyes over her brother's broad shoulder. She clung, her arms around his middle, to the belt of his leather jacket as they swung to the right, banking so steeply she was sure he would have to scrape his steel-soled shoe to keep them from going over.

A ride behind Jack on the big motorcycle always

I

brought a mixture of joy and terror. He didn't ask her often, so she always felt it was a privilege, and it *was* fun, but mostly in thinking about it afterward. Each time he asked she would forget about the engine, the whipping wind, the frantic clasp to keep from flying off on the curves and dips. She would be so thrilled that her big brother was willing to take her with him that she could only climb aboard and hang on for her life. Besides, he never really gave her a choice. When he wanted her to go with him he merely drove up to her, twisted his head to the side, shot a quick glance at her and then at the rear of his cycle. It seemed like a command, and there had never been a time when she had refused.

So now, her chin pressed against his shoulder, his long hair and hers streaming together, she watched in horror as the cycle rushed at the back of the tank truck grinding up the hill ahead of them, swung wildly into the other lane, roared past the dark bulk, and whipped in ahead of it, just in time to dodge an oncoming car, the driver open-mouthed in horror at the narrow margin which Jack liked to play with.

As the meadows of Lacy Flats opened ahead where the road for a half mile split Lacy's farm clean into two balanced pieces, Sue managed one timid glance at the speedometer—seventy-eight miles an hour. It's better not to know, she decided, as the Lacy house swished past on one side and the barn on the other. She knew that someone was waving, but she didn't dare unclasp a single finger from her grip on Jack's belt to return it. The Lacys would understand anyway because it had hap-

pened before. Besides, Sue had her mind on the cycle's
thin rear tire which Jack had just patched, and that was
enough to worry about—that and whether he was ever
going to slow down to make the turn into their drive.

At the last minute, with a catch of brakes which
pressed Sue even flatter against his back, Jack swerved
into the gravel yard with a spray of stones, shut off the
engine while they were still moving ahead, and came to
a silent stop within inches of the trailer door.

Sue breathed, "Thanks, Jack," and slid off, holding onto the doorknob, not trusting her trembling legs
to support her at first. She took the two steps to the sofa,
flopped down full length, and let the tightness go out of
her. After all, she was still alive. She knew that the next
time he beckoned she'd go again.

She watched lazily as Jack strolled in and poured
himself a cup of coffee. He stood up to drink it, stooping
forward to peer out of the window.

"Ford panel truck—'61 or '62—heavy-duty back
springs," he muttered. "What's *he* want?"

Sue lifted her head and saw a thin, gray-haired
stranger emerge from the vehicle, looking back and forth
from the house to the trailer, uncertain where to go, not
seeing the eyes watching him from both. He came
toward the trailer and called, "Anybody home? This's
where Bill Servey lives, ain't it?"

"Not home," said Jack, and Sue stood behind him
in the doorway, on tiptoes, glancing over his shoulders,
almost as if they were still on the Harley. She was sure

3

that she had never seen this little man in overalls, and yet something about his face *was* familiar.

"Up here, Fred." Bill Servey appeared on the porch of the house, waving. "What's it take to bring you sixty miles for the first time in twelve years?"

"Susan and Jack, shake hands with your Uncle Fred. He doesn't give us many chances to see him so we'll get him while he's here. Come on up here, Fred. Old Gore will want to see you, but he isn't getting up 'cause his ribs are busted. Come on, now, you're just in time to join us for our mid-morning coffee break."

The "living room" of Gore's house was the only room. It was kitchen, bedroom, dining room, and living room combined—everything but bathroom, which was outside. Gore, grizzly with several days' growth of gray whiskers as usual, lay back on the sofa. He was shirtless, his chest bandaged and strapped.

"This serious?" Fred asked him.

"No," scoffed Gore. "It's just that the older I get the more I seem to stumble and get off balance. Then I fall into things on the side where I don't have an arm to stop myself. Some of these ribs have been broken three times now. They heal in a while. In the meantime all they do is hurt every time I breathe. Don't tell any jokes because it about kills me to laugh."

"I don't know of anything funny," Fred told them, and he looked as if he hadn't laughed in a long time. Although he was the youngest of his brothers, the deep lines of worry on his thin face made him look older than Bill or Gore.

4

The three Servey brothers, together for the first time since Bill and Gore had left the mine twelve years ago and come to Oakton, talked about old times and about friends the two had not seen since then. Fred told them that three years after the two brothers left, the mines opened up for a couple of years and then closed completely.

"More miners left after that," Fred told them. "About one family out of three took off. God knows where they went—some to the city, some up to the orchard country to work part-time. Some of them figured on coming back but none ever did. And of course all the young people left if they could.

"I worked at logging for a time, then back at the pit when the mine reopened. When it shut down the last time it shut tight. Of course there's always talk that it will start up again. Politicians were always promising us they'd get things going, and that's why I stayed, you know how it is. They said that the power company was planning on putting in a big steam turbine generator right at the mine mouth where they could get the coal without any transportation costs, but nothing ever happened."

"So what are you doing now?" asked Gore.

"I'm up here to see if I can work a deal that may help us all," Fred answered. "I'll tell it to you all at once and you see what you think of it."

"Wait till I get another cup of coffee," Bill said. "I can't listen to a story without a cup of coffee."

"It's a short story," Fred told him. "My wife's

brother got me a job in Eli, just a few miles from here. I'm a janitor at the school where he works. It's not much money, but I can't complain since it's the first job I've had in three years. I start Monday.

"Now I have to be there early in the day because I'm also supposed to drive a school bus. I can't go back home sixty miles every night, and I can't bring Nan and the kids here until I've got a place for them to stay in. So what I want to know is, can I put up a shack on your place and bring my family up here when it's finished? As soon as we can afford a bigger house we'll move out and you can have the shack."

Bill Servey poured more coffee into Fred's half-filled cup. Gore lay on the sofa puffing on his pipe. A moment of silence came and left, interrupted by a sigh.

"What do you say, Bill?" asked Gore from the sofa.

"I say there's plenty of room here, but it's your place."

"Fred, there's only one thing that bothers me," said Gore. "I just hope that your job doesn't peter out right off. We've got a little junk business here and we pick up trash around town. We don't have much but we're making out okay. Now we can't support two more adults and six kids on this kind of money no matter how hard we try."

"Oh, no! Oh, my no!" Fred assured them. "This job is a sure thing. And as soon as we can save up enough to rent us a place in town, we'll do it, 'cause that's what Nan really wants."

6

"When do you want to start building?" asked Gore.

"Right now. I've got the measurements with me, and I brought a shovel and a pickax. If you'll show me where I can build, I'll start to level the ground right now."

"Pick it out yourself," Gore told him. "You know what you want better than we do. We get water from a spring just in back of Bill's trailer. There's plenty there for you to pipe to your place if you want to."

Bill winked at Sue. "Now you won't be the only woman in the family. We'll have somebody else to boss us around when your Aunt Nan gets here."

Sue smiled and nodded and wondered how it would all work out. She could think of reasons against and reasons for being the only girl on the place.

2.

Uncle Fred came again on Monday night, his panel truck crammed full of old boards and two by fours. He set to work at once but he explained that he would have to erect the house a little differently from the usual manner.

"I'm taking down one of the company shacks," he told them. "Nobody is using it any more and it will just fall to pieces in a few years unless somebody takes care of it. So I'm tearing it down and bringing it up here to put together again. But when you tear a place down you have to take the roof off and then the walls before you

8

can get to the floor and the sills, which is the opposite from the way you build. I can't start with the roof when I'm putting it back together, but I'm trying to assemble some of the wall sections here so that I can set them in place when I finally get the floor boards and sills."

Sue watched the building's progress, but homework took so much of her time—homework from school and real home work—that she made only what amounted to an inspection trip each afternoon. Uncle Fred had brought a long extension cord and a light, and she could hear him hammering after she had gone to bed.

She wondered at night, in the only time there was to wonder, what her cousins would be like. She had been the only "woman" in the household for so long she had become accustomed to it, and she wasn't even sure that she was happy about the prospect of Aunt Nan and her six children, three of them girls, moving in.

Things seemed to be taking care of themselves pretty well under their present living conditions. Since Mom had died years ago, Dad had done the cooking, Jack did the dishes usually, and Sue attended to the washing and ironing and most of the cleaning. Uncle Gore, up in the house, took care of himself, and he liked it that way. He always ate breakfast with them but preferred to prepare his other two meals and eat alone, except for coffee breaks, which were always held at his house.

"In my home I'm boss," Uncle Gore frequently stated, and he seemed to feel that the only way he could always maintain that top-notch position was to live alone. At any rate, there was no one with whom he had to argue about it.

The little compound of Serveys, three living in the trailer and one in the house, managed to get along pretty well together. The best explanation would probably be that they all had a deep-rooted belief in independence that amounted to a religion with them. "If you want independence you've got to be willing to let the other guy have his," was the Servey creed.

The only real, long-standing argument was between Jack and his father over whether Jack could drop out of high school.

"I don't need a high school diploma to be in the junk business," Jack maintained on every occasion that the subject arose.

"Well, there's no money in the junk business," Bill would always reply. "You may want to do something better as you get older, and without a diploma you're stuck."

"There's nothing wrong with this business," Jack would say, and his father would answer, "There's nothing dishonest about it, no, and nothing to be ashamed of, but there's no money in it and no future in it. Now in two more years you'll be through. Just stick to it and someday you'll be glad you did, believe me."

And so Jack plodded along reluctantly into his junior year at Monton High. He brought home a warning or two about his grades but somehow managed to keep from "going down the drain," as he expressed it. Bill was proud that Jack never attempted to take the easy path of flunking his subjects and thus being forced out of school.

Uncle Fred was easy enough to get along with. While he was building his home he ate with Gore and slept on a cot in the back of his panel truck. By the time cold weather arrived in late October the shack was up, and although it was not finished, it was done enough for him to stay in nights.

"It seems funny having a company shack on the place after all these years," Bill often remarked. "Just look at the size of that thing. That is what ten thousand miners working for the Mountain Coal Company had to call home, most of them all their lives. There's two rooms, and neither one of them is any bigger than the rooms in our trailer. And the company expected you to raise a family of six or eight kids in a place like that."

"They didn't want us to live in 'em," Gore said. "They wanted us to live in the mine. They wanted us to go down in the pit about the time the sun came up and come out when it was getting dark. No, we weren't supposed to live in those shacks, just eat and sleep there, and live in the mine."

"Remember how they used to give us all the no-good coal to burn in our stoves?" Bill asked. "How I miss that yellow smoke curling up out of the chimney. Or more likely curling up out of the stove and into the house because it was so hard to get any heat out of it."

"I wonder if any company official ever looked inside one of those shacks," said Gore. "I wonder what one of them would ever say if he had to stay with six kids for just one night in a place that size in the summer with the temperature a hundred and ten all night and in the winter with the wind breezing right in one side and out the other because they were all made cheap and quick with green lumber."

But Fred worked every weekday night, and by November the shack had been completely reassembled. A "mobilehome" they called it—a house that had wandered sixty miles off its foundations. And it was better than it had been when it was first built. Fred had replaced all of the windows and, with Jack's help, had put plasterboard on the walls and ceiling.

"It's really not much of a place for eight people," he admitted, "but it's no smaller than what we're living in now, and I only aim to keep the family here until I can save up enough to find a bigger place."

On a Thursday evening in mid-November he surveyed his handiwork and told Bill and Gore, "Tomorrow night I'm going home and start loading furniture. Over the weekend I'll make a couple of trips up here bringing furniture, and on Sunday night we're going to move in!"

But though Bill and Gore and Jack and Sue watched all day Saturday and again on Sunday, Uncle Fred did not return. On Monday in the late afternoon his truck drove in the yard, but he was alone.

"She wouldn't come," he told them. "Nan says that she's lived all her life in a miner's shack and she isn't going to move to another one. She wants to go to the city and start a new life there. I can't seem to change her mind. So I guess you've got yourself a new house, if you want it."

"Argue her out of it," said Gore. "She'll never find an easy life in the city any more than she will here."

"I've tried," Fred said shaking his head, "but I can't get anywhere. After all, I've asked a lot of her all these years and maybe this is too much. Maybe I'd better try the city and see how it works out."

"When she gets fed up with her 'new life,'" Gore told him, "come back here. Your place will be waiting for you. Of course you'll have to find work again because you'll lose the janitor's job."

"Maybe I'll find a good job in the city. Maybe I'll make enough money so that we can rent a house, the way Nan wants to, if we ever come back here," said Fred.

"Maybe," said Gore as Fred drove away, "but no coal miner I ever knew got rich by moving to the city."

Sue's closest friend was Janet Lacy, who lived at the farm just down the road. Both girls had home chores to do during weekends so there wasn't much time for play, but for years they had been "talking friends." Now in the seventh grade there seemed to be more than ever that needed talking about.

Janet's father had recently fixed a room for her in the attic of the big farmhouse. No one but her mother could understand why she wanted to be up there where it was usually cold in winter and hot in summer, and where she had to climb an extra flight of stairs. But it was the perfect place for a girl to be by herself, away from her brothers. It was also the perfect place for two girls to reveal their secret thoughts to each other.

On a Saturday afternoon Sue and Janet lay in identical positions on their stomachs, elbows out, chins on hands, looking out of the window between the iron rungs at the head of Janet's bed. A December snow was sinking away from them in their high perch, large flakes floating down from nowhere and falling to lose themselves in the white mass on the ground.

"I wish I had a room like this, so high up," Sue spoke almost in a whisper to match the quiet of the time. "I love looking down on everything—seeing the tops of things, and people not knowing that you're watching them."

"I know. It's not like spying on people, it's sort of being with them without having to say anything or do anything." Janet kicked her shoes off onto the floor. "I love this room better than any place in the world. It's almost like being in a tower in a castle where a princess might live looking out at the countryside below."

"There's nothing like this in a trailer, you can bet."

"No, but I like the way you folks live too. There's independence to it. Take your Uncle Gore. He lives by himself. Our uncle stays with us because the house is so big, and he's in our hair all the time. He isn't so bad, but it's just that he's always around.

"And this place is all part of the farm. They have

to go together. You folks can work less of the time and still make out all right. Living in this house means living on this farm, and that means working almost all the time. My folks never sit down and drink coffee and talk in the middle of a Saturday morning the way your dad and Gore do."

"I guess almost every kind of life has some good things and some bad things about it," Sue thought aloud, "if you look hard enough."

"Let's go and build a snowman." Janet jumped up and began fumbling for her shoes.

"A dragon," called Sue, muffled as she slipped her sweater over her head, "a dragon to guard your castle."

"Crouching, so it will be easy to make," Janet, hopping on one foot back to the bed, her other shoe jerking along behind her. "I forgot I had tied these together."

"A long tail, with scaly ridges."

"And red eyes. Take these buttons to stick in."

Christmas had never seemed very special since Mrs. Servey had died. In fact it seemed as if Jack and Bill had held back, perhaps afraid to have too much fun, thinking that no Christmas should be better than their last together. Bill always roasted a turkey and baked mince pie, they always invited Gore down to the trailer for dinner, they had a tree and gave each other presents, but always with a little holding back, a kind of reserve of pleasure not to be spent.

This year there was something in the wind. When Sue was not with them Jack would say to his father, "You sure there's nothing mean about it? For that price there must be something wrong."

"Never look an almost gift horse in the mouth," was the only answer Bill Servey would give him.

And Gore, over his coffee cup up at the house, "The expense doesn't end with the buying, you know. You're going to have to get more to go with it."

"I know, but I've spent little enough on her. She's the only girl I've got."

"She's the only girl we've got between us. Let me chip in fifty-fifty with you."

"You sure you want to do that?"

"What else have I got to spend it on? Besides, we'll pick up a lot of that in Christmas bonuses on the trash route. That, and I'll go without a couple of bottles— which won't kill me, though it may come close to it."

Sue sensed that something special was going on. No one had dropped the least bit of a hint, yet there was a feeling of expectancy. It did her no good to ask Jack. He kept almost everything secret anyway, so he was in practice for Christmas.

Besides, Jack had a perfect way of stopping her questions. He would ask, "Do you really want to know?"

And of course, although she hoped for a hint which would give her some ideas to build on, she really didn't want to know.

As the time neared, Bill Servey began to worry about some of the things which hadn't concerned him before the deal had gone through. "Looks sound as a dollar," he said to Gore a dozen times. "Can't see why the price is so reasonable unless there's *something* wrong."

"You going to keep this a secret right up to the end?"

"Until Christmas morning, if I can."

"It'll take some doing."

"I'll need help."

"Anything I can do, just say the word."

The school Christmas show came and went without making much impression on the family in the trailer. Sue didn't sing very well and so was relegated to a small part. Jack, in his third year as member of the bass section of the high school chorus, never tolerated anyone talking about his singing. As far as the family was concerned, music was his private affair. Bill seldom went to anything, both because his bad back left him exhausted at the end of a working day and because he felt uncomfortable among many of the parents who came to school performances. He didn't own a suit and he couldn't afford one. He didn't want one and wouldn't have worn it if someone gave him one. Gore never left his house in the evenings. Thus neither of them attended, but neither Sue nor Jack was bothered by it.

What Sue really wanted to get her father was a heating pad for his back, but the cheapest was $7.95, far beyond her means. She had settled for some shaving soap without much enthusiasm. Then Jack told her that he couldn't think of anything to get, so they pooled their cash and found that they could afford the pad, with Jack paying the $7.00 and Sue the 95¢.

In home economics class Sue made liners for Jack's leather mittens. For Gore she knitted warm socks, as she had done for the past two years. The ability to knit was one of the last gifts she had received at the age of eight from her dying mother.

School was held until noon of the day before Christmas, and during the afternoon Sue stayed in town with Janet to help with her shopping. Since Sue had accounted for all of her gifts and didn't have a single penny left to spend, she enjoyed Janet's shopping as if it were her own. The Lacys, though they didn't live in a trailer and have a trash route, were nearly as poor as the Serveys. Only the wisest of spending could supply presents for a family from Janet's meager hoard of nickels and dimes.

In the late afternoon they walked the two miles from town to Janet's house. Sue was invited to stay for dinner, as frequently happened. The only thing unusual about the event, and it did puzzle her for a while until she just gave up thinking about it, was that when she said that she should run home first and ask Dad, Mr. Lacy said that Bill had already said it would be all right.

Later, in the "tower room." where she insisted on taking Sue "for a few minutes" before she went home, Janet asked, "What is your dad going to give you?"

"I don't know, but there's something up. Usually he hints and tries to get me to guess, and usually it's something in a box under the tree ahead of time, but this

year he hasn't said a thing. He acts as if he wants me to
think he's forgotten it altogether. I just can't figure it."

"It may be something big," suggested Janet with
a smile, and suddenly Sue realized that her friend knew.

"Don't you tell me!"

Janet laughed. "Don't worry, I'm not going to say
anything. But what would you want if you could have
your wish of anything in the world?"

"Of anything?"

"Sure, no matter what it cost."

"Well, you know what I want—what I've wanted
for as long as I can remember. I want a horse—a chestnut
mare with a saddle and bridle and a barnful of hay and
a barrel full of oats, and a horsetrailer to haul her around
to shows, and a blanket to keep . . . Say, look, I didn't
realize you can see our place so well from your window.
Sue, a car or a truck just pulled into our driveway. There
comes Gore out with a flashlight, and that must be either
Jack or Dad."

"You're not supposed to be spying on the people
next door," laughed Janet. "It's not polite."

"We ought to arrange a signal system sometime.
I could flash a light out of my window and I'll bet you
could see it. Look, they're going to unload that truck.
Imagine bringing junk for us to have to look over on the
night before Christmas. I hope Dad tells him to take it
out to the dump."

"Come on away from that window," said Janet
pulling the blind down. "I'll report you as a peeping
Tom."

"Peeping Toms look *in* people's windows, not out."

"Well, anyway, there's no sense in your going home now, everybody's busy. Stay a while and help me wrap presents."

3.

In the night Sue dreamed of a chestnut mare. In the dream she rode the mare in the ring at the Arlingham horse show and they took the jumps beautifully, one after another, while a spellbound audience applauded each round. At the end of the course she reined in the mare sharply, causing her to rear up on her hind legs and neigh so loudly that Sue woke with a start and nearly fell out of bed. The dream was so real and the sound at the end so startling that she had trouble getting back to sleep.

In the morning there was breakfast still with an air of expectancy. There was nothing yet for Sue under the tree, and no hints. Gore came down from the house, and they ate slowly, the men sipping their coffee as if nothing were about to happen.

"It's time for presents," Sue announced firmly.

"I didn't see any there for you," Gore said, raising his eyebrows and looking from face to face around the table.

For a moment she wondered and thought that perhaps they *had* forgotten, or had not been able to afford anything. After all, Christmas didn't seem to mean much to Gore. He just watched and never gave anyone anything. And her father these past few years had never seemed very interested. Tears found their way into her eyes although she fought them back.

Then the silence was broken by a shrill whinny, and Sue felt as if her whole being was charged with electricity.

"I heard that in the night," she gasped, "and I thought that it was part of my dream." She looked at her father.

"Better go out to the shed and see what it is."

In a single motion the girl left the table and lunged out of the trailer, the sound of falling chair and slamming door behind her, and her father's call, "In the shed."

In her slippers, without even a sweater, she raced across the icy yard and up to the old junk shed. She threw open the door, and there, where only a day ago had been stacks of gears and steel beams, and axles, a horse stall had been fashioned and a horse's head was peering anxiously over the newly made stall door. Sue stood in the doorway and a shiver ran down her spine. The horse nodded its head up and down several times, as if to say, "Yes, I'm yours," and then pawed the floor impatiently, striking the stall door with the front of its hoof as it did so.

Sue moved toward the animal in wonder and glory, and saw that there was a red ribbon around its neck with a card. She patted the creature's nose and reached for the card. It said, "A chestnut mare for Sue, from Jack and Bill and Gore," and Gore was underlined. Her eyes saw it dimly because they were full of tears, but her whole being saw it and kept the words and the underline forever. And when the three men came in, after giving her a few minutes to be alone with her gift, they found her in the stall with her arms around the mare's neck, her face pressed tight against it.

She turned to them, tears streaming down her face, and they knew that this girl who had wanted so badly and never asked had been holding back more than they had realized. She tried to smile, and she tried to thank them but she couldn't, and they understood and left her alone in the stall with the chestnut mare.

Later she came back to the breakfast table and sat down with them, and then they could talk, although the men could see that it was not easy for Sue to control her voice. Her father explained that the mare had been left in the care of one of his friends in the late fall by some summer people. Bill's friend had kept it in his barn, and then received word from the owners to sell the mare and the saddle and bridle.

"It took me a while before I realized that there was a saddle hanging in the shed, too."

"Mare's not much use without a saddle," her father commented. "Now, Sue, I didn't know how much this would mean to you, and it doesn't make any sense to say don't get your hopes up too high. But I want to warn you, we didn't pay the regular horse price for that mare. We couldn't have bought her at the going rate. But whenever a horse is low in price it usually means there's something to look out for. I haven't found it yet, but at least I'm satisfied that she isn't mean and won't hurt you. That's the thing I'm most concerned about."

"But what kind of things could be wrong?" asked Sue, already worried about the health of her mare.

"Well, she could have a lame leg, one that gets sore after a little riding, or she could be foundered. But if you treat her good and don't ride her too hard, she should be horse enough for you. And it wouldn't hurt to read up a little on horse care."

"When can I ride her?"

"Now brace yourself, Sue, because the yard is all ice now, and in the fields all the woodchuck holes are hidden by snow. You're just going to have to wait about three months until the end of March or the beginning of April. And we can't put up any fence until the ground thaws so we can drive in fenceposts. You'll have to exercise your mare a little each day by leading her around the yard."

"My mare," Sue murmured, loving the sound of the words.

"I didn't realize it would mean so much to you. I guess it's pretty hard on a girl living in a trailer down here at the junkyard. Us men don't give it much thought."

Sue looked at her father. "I don't mind living here. We've got a better family than lots of people because we like each other. And this trailer is better than plenty of the houses that kids in my class live in. The trailer is small, but it's modern and it's built right for living in. And as far as being in the junk business and collecting trash, sure some kids are nasty about it, but they're nasty anyway. The rest of the kids don't care what you do for a living.

"And now," she finished, "I'll be the only one in my class to have a riding horse. Imagine me, owning a chestnut mare."

Breakfast was finished and cleared away. The rest of the presents came next. When Bill Servey discovered his heating pad he exclaimed, "Well, I'd look foolish hugging this, but I reckon I'm about as glad to get it as you are that horse. If this really fixes my back so that I can sleep nights, I'll be a new man. Maybe that coal mine didn't ruin me after all."

Gore's gift from Jack had to be demonstrated. It

was something the boy had made after hours at the school woodworking shop.

"You see," he showed Gore, "it works like this. You put your log down in the sawbuck here and then you just flip this clamp over to hold it. It's made special for a one-armed man so he can saw wood easy."

"Well, I'll be darned!" Gore was touched by the gift. "I never figured there was a way to make life easy for a one-armed man. And you went and invented this yourself. Well, I'll be darned."

And so on Christmas morning, Gore set about cutting stove wood so as to enjoy his especially designed sawbuck; Bill lay down on the sofa to try out his new heating pad; Jack drove off on his motorcycle using his new mitten liners; and Sue returned to the shed to whisper secrets to her beloved chestnut mare.

Two minutes later she raced back into the trailer, breathless.

"What's the matter, child?" her father raised his head from his drowsy position on the sofa.

"What's her name? I suddenly realized that I never asked her name."

"Houri," Bill lay back smiling. "She's part Arabian and part quarter horse. I've got papers on her. And her name is Houri Dawn."

4.

In the attic, sprawled on the bed, Janet Lacy and Sue Servey surveyed the small piece of the world which lay below them. Janet's younger brother, red-haired and freckled as she was, worked hatless at clearing a path to the spring house. A dozen heifers loose in the small pasture milled about with no purpose. Beyond were snow-laden fields, a strip of woods, and then the Serveys' place.

"You knew about the mare, didn't you?" Sue asked.

"Somebody had to keep you away from home that afternoon so that Jack could finish making a stall. As it turned out you were such a peeping Tom you saw the truck come to deliver her."

"I never dreamed what I was seeing."

"I was beginning to get worried when they started to unload the truck."

"I wouldn't have believed that they would all give me a horse even if I had seen one unloaded. In fact, I thought I knew about those men in the family. Now I know there's more to them than I understood."

"Look," Janet said, suddenly noticing. "What in the world is Gore doing to his house?"

"Taking the front off so he can drive the trash truck in."

"What do you mean, drive the trash truck in?"

"Just that. It needs a motor overhaul, he says—connecting rod or something like that. It's a big job and it's too cold to work on it outdoors. So he's going to work on it inside. He moved his cot way out to the back and he's put some heavy planks on the floor so the wheels won't break through. There's no cellar anyway. And he measured and says there's just room without moving the stove."

"Well, you just can't take a wall out of your house, you know!" Janet sputtered.

"Uncle Gore can. He's cutting out a piece just the right size to drive the truck through, and he's putting it on hinges so that he can open and close it anytime."

28

"But who ever heard of a truck in the house?" asked Janet hopelessly.

Sue told her, "Uncle Gore doesn't ask anybody if a thing is all right before he goes ahead and does it. It's his house and if he wants to drive a truck in it, he'll do it. In fact," she added, "I think that's one of the things I like most about him."

Houri was a delight. Sue visited with her in the morning before she left for school and always as soon as she came home, and one last time before going to bed. Janet came often, and a few of the girls from school visited the mare and sighed in envy, begging for rides later when the ground would be thawed.

During a January thaw Bill showed her how to use a lead line, and to their delight they discovered that the mare had been trained to one. She would walk or trot on command, and Bill was sure that she would canter if called to, but was afraid that there might still be a patch of ice on which she would slip.

February was bitter cold with little promise of the spring which should be coming, and March announced its arrival with a blizzard. In the midst of this worst snowstorm of the year, just as the supper table was being cleared, there was a knock at the door, and Uncle Fred entered. That is, it looked like Uncle Fred, but even thinner and much older than when he had left in November.

"Fred," said Bill Servey, half rising from his place at the table, "is your family with you?"

"I've come back alone," was his rasping reply.

"Well, sit down, man. Jack, put the food back on the table—open up a can of hash. Sue, go and get your Uncle Gore. He'll want to come right down."

Fred Servey removed the snow-covered coat, revealing its tattered lining. He looked small, even in the trailer. Sue dashed past him toward Gore's house.

"Fred's back."

"Alone?"

"Yes. He doesn't look well."

Gore slipped his one arm into his coat and they hurried down to the trailer.

They crowded in the small living-dining room of the trailer, Fred wolfing down great forkfuls of leftover potatoes and beans, alternated with long draughts from the coffee mug. Jack, in the kitchenette, stirred a pan of hash, then brought it out, steaming.

No one asked Fred any more questions, since it would not have been right to interrupt the meal of which he was so obviously in need. Finally he stopped and pushed the plate away. Gore offered him a cigarette, which he took, and Bill lit it for him. He leaned back and blew smoke into the air for a moment, then began speaking in his raspy, croaky voice.

"No man knows better than I do now that when all you've done is work in the coal mines you're not much good for anything else. I didn't want to go to the city. I only went there because Nan wanted me to. But

I was fool enough to think that we could start a new life there.

"A man with no education and no skill at any job except mining doesn't get far these days. Why there's young men, strong men, smart men out of work in the city. I took any job I could find—sweeping, washing dishes, lifting and carrying—anything anybody'd give me to do. Most of the jobs would only last a week or two 'cause I'd be taking somebody's place while they were sick or on vacation. And most everything that has any pay to it is unionized.

"But no matter how hard I worked I never could make enough for us to live on. And you should see the places they make you pay rent for—high rent too. Walk up four flights, one room and share a kitchen with two other families, and a bathroom down the hall. No hot water ever except what you heat on the little stove if two or three other people aren't waiting to use it. I tell you, it was plenty worse than those company shacks we've always complained about."

"How did Nan take it?" asked Bill.

"She didn't say much at first, since she brought it on. But what hurt her worse than anything, maybe next to the rats and bugs in those buildings, was that the kids didn't have any place to play but in the streets. And you never saw such tough kids as they had to play with. Our kids were getting beat up all the time. It's like a jungle.

"And then we couldn't pay our bills. I had to sell the truck, but there wasn't anyplace to park it in the streets anyway. That money didn't last long because I

31

didn't get much for it. We bought some furniture, just a little, when we first got to town, and I was paying on the installment plan. Well, I couldn't keep it up and so they sent some men and took it away. I tell you it's hard to watch them take your sofa and chairs right out of your house, and you not able to do anything about it.

"Well, I kept trying to find better work and to make more money, but there just wasn't anything. Then came the last straw and that's when I left. We'd applied for welfare but we could only get a tiny bit because we hadn't lived there long enough to qualify. But last week Nan found out about a kind of welfare that pays a certain amount for each child you've got. She found out that she could get more money that way than I was making in my little two-bit jobs. The only trouble is you can only get it if the husband isn't living with the family. He has to have deserted them.

"Now, mind you, our kids were hungry. We weren't eating regular on what I was making. So there wasn't anything for me to do but leave my family so they could have enough welfare money to live on. I'm worth more to them if I stay away than I am if I try to make money for them."

His story told, Fred leaned forward with his hands over his face. He stayed that way for a minute while the rest sat in stunned silence. Then gradually his hands fell away, his mouth fell open, and he slept.

"Like a baby," breathed Gore.

Bill said, "He's probably been walking and hitch-hiking. And knowing him, I'll bet he left every cent with his family. He didn't look as if he'd eaten in days, and you know how sleepy that makes you."

"Carry him up to my place," said Gore.

"No, let him lie right there. We'll just stretch him out on my sofa. I don't have the heart to move him even if that sofa is the best bed I ever slept on in my life. For once it won't hurt me to give it up to a man that's tireder than I am. I'll stay up at your place."

"Bill, isn't that the saddest thing you ever heard in your life?"

Bill shook his head. "I don't know of anything in this world that could hurt a man more than being worth more to his family if he left them than he would be if he stayed."

"Isn't that the truth! But you know darn well you wouldn't have let your wife get you in a mess like that."

"But Ma wasn't uppity like Aunt Nan, was she, Dad?" asked Sue.

"No, and Fred always wanted to give Nan a chance to try things her way. Of course what he should have seen was that once they'd got in trouble like that there'd be no way of getting out."

Jack had been staring at Uncle Fred, finding it unbelievable that a grown man could pass out and lie sound asleep in a room while people talked about him. "What will he do now?" he whispered.

"We'll have to wait until we can talk it over tomorrow," his father told him. "Throw a blanket over him, Jack, and let's go up to Gore's house."

33

"I'll stay here," volunteered Sue. "Somebody ought to look after him." She spent the evening watching and more than once she wept, for to Sue Servey the saddest thing that could happen was for a family to separate.

5.

Fred Servey was sick for two weeks, and there were times when no one was sure whether he would live. Bill and Gore knew that if they called a doctor he would move Fred to a hospital at once, and that no one, least of all Fred, could afford it. So they gave him day and night care, with someone at his bedside constantly. Medication varied from hot coffee to hot whiskey to hot soup to hot mustard plaster.

"At least," announced Bill, "we're not foolish enough to try anything cold."

35

In the end he survived, whether because of the medication or in spite of it, though he was so weakened that he could barely stand. He spent another two weeks hobbling about in the yard enjoying the late March sunshine, and then went up to live in his transplanted miner's shack. No one asked him what he planned to do because it was clear that he was unable as yet to do anything except regain his health.

For Sue, the coming of the warm March days meant a chance at last to ride her beloved Houri. Bill and Gore had begun setting fenceposts to mark out a pasture. Gore had salvaged about a half-mile of barbed wire which someone had thrown in the trash.

"You do your riding inside the fence until you get the hang of it," her father told her.

Houri had been groomed at least twice a week ever since Christmas, the saddle had been soaped and the stirrups polished a dozen times.

"You'll have everything worn out before you even get to use it," Jack told her.

"I don't spend any more time keeping my horse and equipment in shape than you do working on your blessed motorcycle."

April came in warmth and mist and lovely hope, and now the fence was finished and the chestnut mare could at last be ridden.

Of a sudden, there was fear in Sue's expectancy. I'll fall off, she said to herself, or Houri will resent a poor rider and throw me off. And I'll look foolish, anyway, not knowing what to do.

She had read everything in the library on horses and riding. Most of it had seemed either too simple or too difficult. But as usual, her father was there to save the day. He was not a rider but he had spent years at the mine and in the woods working around horses, and he understood them, as they did him.

And so the great adventure began with Bill giving his daughter the assurance she needed and leading Houri around the pasture with first a short, then a long lead line. It was discovered rather quickly that the mare had been trained to neck rein, and before the first session was over, Sue was able to turn by herself while her father watched from a short distance. She was content, and so was he, that this first lesson be an introduction more than anything else, and a building up of confidence between rider and horse.

That evening Sue walked alone to the top of the hill behind the trailer. She sat there, hugging her knees in this quiet place in the cool of early April, deeply moved and grateful that the powerful animal had been eager to follow her fragile commands. She said aloud, yet to herself, "Houri could have done anything, yet she did just what I asked of her."

The motorcycle, ordinarily a roar, from this distance was a hum, the single light flickered between the trees as Jack hurtled along the road to home. "No place to go, only speed to get there," her father always said. The light turned into the yard and Jack gunned the engine in his customary manner before letting it rest in well-earned silence.

Below, the lights shone in the trailer and the miner's shack. Gore must be visiting with Bill and hadn't returned to the house yet. This peaceful little gathering of buildings was like the Chinese compound she had read about. To the Chinese the family was everything—sacred like a religion. Perhaps they were right, because it didn't seem as if anything else had the same strength to hold people together. Where else in the world was there to go but home? Home is where they take you in because you belong there.

The wooden fence along the road, barely visible in the fading light, completed the resemblance to a compound. State law required the owners of any junkyard to build a board fence screening it from the road. She thought of Uncle Fred, his family, fenced out, not in the compound where their struggles bound them together and gave their lives purpose. Perhaps Nan would be tired of city life and someday return. Yet it seemed as if Fred had given up hope. He had done nothing more to the inside of the shack, which was as yet unfinished, and he had not been able to find a job. Sue resolved that if she could ever help to bring the man and his wife and children together, she would do so. For purely selfish reasons she was not sure that she really looked forward to having another woman in the compound, especially one with a number of younger children, but one look at what the family split had done to Fred was enough to show that the healing was a need greater than any other.

She saw the trailer door open, throwing a ray of light into the night.

She could barely hear her father call her name. She rose and answered knowing that he would call back, "Bedtime."

During the next week Sue saddled Houri and rode her in the pasture each night after school. Janet came to watch twice but declined the offer of a ride.

"It's you two who have to learn to get along," she said.

By Thursday, Sue thought that she was ready to try trotting, but when she did the bouncing motion disconnected her completely and she nearly went off, first one side, then the other, then almost over the mare's head when she slowed to a walk.

"There's something I have to learn about trotting, I guess," she said in what was as mild a statement as could be made on the subject.

On Saturday afternoon her father tried to help her, but he knew no more about trotting than she did, so the session turned into a slightly disappointing walk. It was right then that the entire horse affair took a decidedly new turn.

With a squeal of tires and the throb of a powerful engine, a Jaguar convertible spun into the yard. At the wheel was a girl in oversized dark glasses, her long blond hair in a ponytail. She slipped out of the car and came toward them, striding gracefully in her bluejean shorts. Houri was walking in a lazy circle, so that Sue, in order to watch the approaching girl, had to look first to one side, then over her shoulder, then to the other side.

The girl slipped between the barbed wire strands with a single motion, and Sue thought, she moves as if she could go anywhere and nothing would stand in her way. And as she came closer, she is beautiful, the most beautiful person I have ever seen.

The girl walked up to Sue's father, her long earrings swinging. "Mind if I watch?"

"Well, no," Bill Servey told her, "but there isn't much to see. The only one here that knows anything is the mare. I'm trying to teach Susan to ride when I don't know anything about it myself."

"Then mind if I make a few suggestions?" She asked the question to Bill but she looked at Sue.

"Why, not at all, go ahead, if you know something about it."

She still looked questioningly at Sue, who nodded approval, though with a slight feeling of reluctance.

"Then," said the girl to Sue, "pull in your elbows, lower your hands but tighten your reins, put down your heels. That's right, but more. There, now tighten your knees, get a grip with them. Now pull your elbows in again unless you're trying to fly. Now lift up your chin and straighten your back. There. Now you look like somebody."

Somehow, Sue thought, I *feel* as if I look better.

"Now hold that position and let's see you walk your chestnut mare around that circle again. That's it, keep those elbows in. Chin up now. You don't have to look at her feet. Look out between her ears. Now you're riding. Make her stop. No, still. That's it, and hold her head up, don't let her eat grass. There, motionless. You'll make a horsewoman, with practice."

She turned to Bill and said, "I'll make a deal with the two of you. Let me give this girl riding lessons every Saturday afternoon, and let me ride the mare by myself one afternoon a week. I'll pay you five dollars for that. Does that seem fair?"

"Well," Bill hesitated, "I don't know what to say. It's Sue's mare. What do you think, Sue?"

"I need lessons if I'm going to learn to ride, but . . ."

"I know," the girl told her. "You don't like the idea of somebody else riding your mare. I know how you feel, but don't worry, I'll take good care of her. She's been ridden plenty by other people before now. Look at me. Do you think I'll handle her badly?"

"No," Sue answered, believing herself as she spoke.

"As to the finances . . ." Bill began.

The girl interrupted, "A good hour-and-a-half lesson would cost you plenty. An afternoon's ride would cost me nearly ten dollars. This way we'll break even. But of course you don't know if my lessons will be any good."

"I'd like to try it, Dad," said Sue.

"Suits me, then, and it's your mare." He turned to the girl. "Go easy with her, though. Sue had never ridden before last week." He began walking out of the pasture.

"Glory is my name," the girl called after him.

"And don't worry. I won't make your daughter do anything that's unsafe. I was once a young girl, too, and I wasn't born knowing how to ride."

She turned to Sue. "You ready to shake on it?"

Sue, looking down from the mare, was timid yet determined. "All right," she said, "but maybe before we shake we should see what Houri thinks about you." She began to dismount.

"Not that way," scoffed Glory. "Kick your left foot out of the stirrup and just let yourself slide down from the saddle."

She kicked her sandals off while she held the reins. "It's safer to be barefoot than to wear these."

With one easy, graceful motion she was up in the saddle. And Houri suddenly seemed to act very differently. She was alert, eager, muscles tense, ears forward. Without any apparent movement from Glory, they were off in a canter across the pasture, straight toward the fence and at the last second a quick turn, now bounding in long, reaching strides up the slope and back again, and Houri was trotting a tight circle, breaking out into a figure eight. Glory rode as if she were part of the horse, glued to her back, leaning with her turns, controlling the animal's movements with the slightest urging.

For Sue, it was breathtaking, a revelation of what she had not understood about the relationship between horse and rider. Glory, her blond hair bouncing behind her, was all that Sue wanted to be, and Glory offered her the path to her desire, to become a rider, to move in concert with Houri.

42

They came toward her with a rush, then stopped, motionless. "Now that's a mighty fine little animal you have, there." Glory smiled, a little out of breath, reached forward, and patted Houri's neck. "How, I mean—where—"

"Do you mean how can people who live in a trailer in a junkyard afford a nice horse?" asked Sue.

Glory smiled as she looked down at Sue. "I like people who say what they mean, and you seem to be able to do that better than I."

"Dad and Jack and Gore all put in the money together. They said it wasn't much, and Dad has been worried that there'd be something wrong with her for that price, but we haven't found it."

"There's certainly nothing wrong with her training, nor her wind, nor her legs as far as I can see." Glory dismounted and handed the reins to Sue. Then she went around the mare picking up each hoof and examining it carefully, poking it with a little stick.

"Needs to be shod," she said. "I'll pay for it the first time because I'll be riding her on the road where she needs good shoes." She continued to examine Houri all over, as if she were a horse doctor, Sue thought.

"Now here's something that may be a sign," Glory said, pointing to the mare's back. "See these long scratches? I'll bet your mare is a fence buster. Has she broken out of the pasture yet?"

"Why, no," answered Sue, surprised to have anyone accuse Houri of such a disobedient act.

"That's probably because the fence is new and she

43

hasn't got it loose yet, and she hasn't had the urge to roam this spring. I'll just bet that these are barbed wire scratches and that this wise old scraper knows just how to get a fence loose and then crawl under it. You'll know if you see her someday putting a front hoof up on the lowest wire and pushing it down a bit at a time until it's dangling nice and loose. Then she'll get down so flat you can't believe it's the same beast you've been riding, and she'll crawl under that wire, except that it will scrape her back up some. Isn't that right, Houri? Aren't you just an old freedom-loving fence buster? I'd be, too, if I were a horse. In fact I'm a fence buster anyway," she finished in a quieter tone, not addressing either Sue or the mare.

"Now, my new friend," she said to Sue, reaching out her hand, " are we ready to shake?"

"Oh, yes," said Sue, "I want you to teach me."

"Then get back up there and we'll give us all a workout before we take this creature in for a good rub-down."

It couldn't wait, and Sue had to tell it all to Janet, after supper that night.

"Well, where in the world did she come from? She doesn't sound real. I mean, I believe you, of course, but people like that just don't drop out of nowhere!"

"She didn't drop out of nowhere. She drove a Jaguar," teased Sue.

"Well, you know what I mean. How did she find the place, and all?"

"I asked her that. She said that she had been driv-

44

ing around on back roads looking for somebody who had a horse that she could rent to go riding on. She had seen Houri a couple of days ago out in the pasture, but then she was still looking for a riding stable. When she didn't find one she came back."

"And she drives a Jaguar? How can anybody afford a Jaguar?"

"I guess she has lots of money. She goes to Bickner College. When she left she said she used to live in a trailer summers. Her folks would go on long trips when she was little. Maybe she just said it to make me feel good, but she said she loved living in a trailer."

Janet sighed, "You're lucky. She sounds grand. I don't know why it is that everything happens to you, Sue."

She shrugged her shoulders. "I don't know either. It just happens."

6.

The only job which Fred Servey had been able to get since he had arrived had turned out to be a fizzle, to put it mildly. A printing firm had advertised that they needed another man and he had gone to see them at once. His first assignment had been to crawl inside a large tank and scrape it out. The tank had contained gold paint, and it was stuck on badly. This was an annual cleaning job and one that no one in the factory wanted. Although poor Fred didn't know it, the fact that the tank needed cleaning was the only reason he was hired.

46

And so, on the morning that he began, he was shown the hatchway through which he had to crawl in order to get into the tank. As small as he was, he barely fit through the opening. A fellow worker was stationed outside the tank to hand in tools and to watch after Fred's safety.

That evening when Sue and Jack came home from school they found their father and Gore in the living room of the trailer.

"Why are you home already, Dad?" asked Sue. "There's nothing wrong is there?"

"Fred's in the hospital," he told them.

"Oh, no," cried Sue, stunned. "It just isn't fair for anything more to happen to that poor man."

"Well, it sure has," Gore told her. "If you had seen what he looked like when we went there you . . ."

"Take it easy, Gore. No sense alarming the child. We think he's going to be all right. We're going in later tonight, after supper, and have another look. They're giving him shots and things, and it will take a while to see what reaction they have."

"What happened?" Jack wanted to know.

Gore told the story. "It seems that they hired him to clean out a tank where they'd had gold paint. One of the men was to stay with him, helping and watching out for him. Sometimes there are fumes in those tanks and a person can be overcome if he's sensitive to them.

"Well, Fred got in there and was scraping away and this other fellow stayed around a little while and then walked off, leaving Fred alone without saying anything. Went for a smoke and then got to talking with people and didn't come right back.

"Meantime Fred had begun to get dizzy and then his head started aching. He figured he ought to come out for a while so he called to the fellow to help him. When he didn't get any reply he tried to climb out by himself, but he'd got weak. The fumes were working on him. What's more, he didn't know it but he had an allergy to that gold paint. Some people do, you know, and his hands and wrists were starting to swell up.

"Then he couldn't stand up any longer and he fell, so he got more of the stuff on him, on his hands and knees in the bottom of the tank. He kept his face out of it as long as he could, and he just hollered as long as he was able.

"As luck would have it, the manager of the plant happened to be passing by on his routine rounds, and he heard Fred in the tank. He quick called a couple of men to get a rope, and then he went down into that tank himself and held Fred up until they could lower a rope. So they hauled Fred up through the hatchway and took him to the hospital and gave him emergency treatment."

"It turns out," said Bill, "that the plant manager is allergic to the stuff too, but he wasn't in there long, so he's okay."

After supper the three men left Sue at home while they piled into the trash truck and drove to the hospital. It took her a long time to get started at her chores and homework, because she could not help thinking about Janet's remark about how good things always seemed to happen to Sue. She could not help but wonder if for every good thing that happened there had to be a bad one, or perhaps for every lucky person there must be an unlucky one. The unfairness of this was more than she could bear, and she decided that it could not possibly be true. Yet the terrible pile-up of bad luck that marked the life of Fred Servey was beyond belief, too. She wondered if it were possible to make a move that would reverse the trend and start her Uncle Fred on the way to fortune. She decided that she would do anything that she could to bring this about.

The men came back from the hospital early. "Kicked us out," Gore told her.

"He's going to recover," said Bill, "but that's not all."

"That's enough for now, isn't it?" Sue asked, wondering what else could be important at such a time.

"He's got a job," her father told her. "The plant manager came in while we were there and told Fred that he could have the job of the fellow that ran off and left him in the boiler. They fired that man on the spot, and Fred can have the job as soon as he's well enough to take it. Now, what do you think of that?"

"Wonderful," said Sue, "and I hope that it will be the beginning of a change for him."

They all agreed that it should be.

7.

Wednesday the mare escaped. When Sue and Jack came home from school, Glory was sitting in her car in the yard, reading.

"I've been waiting for you," she said. "Your fence buster is out and I can't find her."

Sue felt a kind of electric shock go through her system.

"Suppose someone has stolen her!"

"That could be, but only if they've found her. I looked the fence over and I found the place she got through. Change out of your school clothes and get in my car. We'll drive around the roads and look for her. We'll need you, Jack, and a rope."

Sue emerged from the trailer in seconds. Jack already had the rope, and the three piled into the car. For one short moment the thought flashed through Sue's mind that she should be thrilled at the chance to ride in a Jaguar, but being thrilled was not quite in keeping with the needs of the moment.

Glory spun the car around in the yard. "Which way?" she asked.

"Well, I wasn't looking very carefully when we came home on the bus, and she could be in that direction but I think we should try the other way first."

"Well, I looked in both directions and didn't see her," said Glory, "but let's try."

The Jaguar shot out into the tarred road with a squeal of tires and roared up the hill to the west. Glory and Sue searched the countryside while Jack's eager eyes ogled the dashboard.

Houri was grazing contentedly in the first field that they came to.

"Must have been behind that hay barn when I came past before," Glory said, disgustedly. She turned the car in at the edge of the road. "You had better approach her, Sue. She knows you best. Hold the rope behind you and walk toward her slowly. She would be easier to catch if we'd remembered to bring a bucket of oats to show her. When you get that snap on her halter, *don't let go.*"

Houri continued to graze, watching Sue's approach out of one eye, casually. As Sue came nearer, the mare stopped grazing and stood watching her. She seemed quietly ready to be led back to her pasture.

Sue talked to her, "Now, Houri, you just stand right still. I'm going to take you home where you belong. Shame on you, breaking loose that way and running off to eat somebody else's grass. Now you just let me get hold of your halter . . ."

At the last second the mare bolted. She wheeled and raced in a circle around the bewildered girl, then kicked her heels to the sky, broke wind, and raced down the road toward home.

Sue's feelings were crushed. Her eyes filled with tears. She turned to Glory and stammered, "She doesn't trust me. She doesn't even like me."

"Nonsense. Get in here and we'll see where she goes. She's just enjoying her freedom, that's all. She's just playing with you and having herself a good time. Look at her tear down that road. Now don't you think she's having the time of her life? There, look, she's heading right in the yard."

With a screech of brakes they turned in almost at her heels, just in time to find a yardful of complete confusion. Bill and Gore had just driven in with the trash truck and were helping Fred, whom they had just brought home from the hospital, across the yard. Houri came straight at them, and the men, caught by surprise, cowered together as if she were going to run into them. Fred gave a scream of panic, thinking that after all his misery, this was the way his end had been planned.

But Houri, incredibly light on her feet, spun to one side, leaped over a box containing Fred's clothing from the hospital, over a pile of trash, and galloped up to her shed. There, to everyone's amazement, she stopped short and calmly began to graze.

Glory was laughing so hard at the whole thing that she nearly ran her Jaguar into the trash truck. Uncle Fred, his face white and his knees shaking, said he didn't see anything funny about it. Sue, afraid that her father would be angry, made her way to Houri, holding the rope behind her back. This time the mare seemed perfectly content to be caught.

"Look at that fresh thing," Glory laughed. "She's smiling, I swear. I believe she's enjoyed every minute of it."

"She sure did look funny tearing straight at those men and scaring them half to death," Sue admitted, smiling. "I would have laughed the way you did, but I didn't dare let Dad or Gore see me."

At that instant Jack started up his motorcycle with a roar. Houri, startled, reared up on her hind legs, jerking the rope out of Sue's hands. In a moment she was off at full speed back through the yard. This time Bill and Gore rushed out into her path, while Fred feebly raced for the porch of Gore's house.

Houri, dodging and twisting, galloped between

53

the two men, the lead rope flailing wildly between her legs. Jack, on his motorcycle, churned up a shower of gravel and dust in the yard as he shot out to the road in pursuit.

Glory ran for her car, calling, "Stay right where you are, Sue. We'll head her your way." She spun the Jaguar around in the yard, but just as she reached the road Houri appeared coming back, hooves clattering on the pavement, with Jack and his motorcycle only a few feet behind her. Glory stopped the car straight across the road, blocking the way and causing the frightened mare to swerve into the yard, again past the men's waving arms.

Glory called, "Open the pasture gate, Sue." And as the mare thundered toward her, Sue swung the gate wide and Houri, neck stretched ahead, tail held high, raced through, a captive at last.

Glory came up, out of breath. "Now would be a good time to give her a small handful of oats," she suggested, "just to show her you're glad she's home. And get that lead rope off her before she stumbles on it. We're lucky she didn't break her neck. She's the most sure-footed creature I ever did see."

From the highway there came a squeal of brakes. "Oh, Lord," cried Glory, "I left the Jaguar parked smack in the middle of the road."

She began to run toward it, but Bill was already there, backing the car into the yard. Luckily there had not been an accident, though the motorist who had barely avoided crashing into the sports car shot an an angry look at them all as he drove past.

"Let's all go in and have some coffee," Bill said, "before anything else happens."

"Right you are," said Glory. "I need to sit down. My knees are shaking."

8.

If Sue had perhaps worried at first about whether her
father and her uncle and brother would embarrass her
by doing or saying the wrong thing in the presence of a
Bickner College girl, she soon found that there was nothing to fear. Glory was very much at ease in the trailer,
as if she had lived with them for years. She joked with
Uncle Gore, and she asked Jack about school. When he
said that he was thinking of dropping out, she encour-
aged him to stay in high school and work for his diploma.

    "There aren't many jobs open to a person who

hasn't graduated from high school," she told him. "Without that diploma you may end up as a . . . a—"

"A trashman," finished Gore. "He'll end up in a junkyard selling old automobile parts and scrap metal, and driving a truck around cleaning up everybody else's mess, just like his father and his uncle."

Before Glory could think of a way out of the predicament in which she had placed herself, Gore went on.

"Now I'll bet you never gave much thought to the trashman's problems, but he has a few besides the fact that a lot of people just don't think he or his kids could be socially acceptable.

"In the first place, he's in business, and he's got to make a profit. You'd be surprised at how eager people are to give you their trash but how reluctant the same people are to part with their cash. They want to put off paying, so I have to carry a notebook around with me to mark down how much they owe. Then there's usually an argument about whether they paid the last time and even if I show them my book, they'll swear I'm mistaken. When people are like that, they're really not dishonest; they just have a habit of remembering to their own advantage.

"Then lots of people who would be embarrassed if the grocery man or the druggist knew they didn't have enough money to pay their bills don't worry much about what the trashman thinks. One woman in town who drives a new car and lives like a queen didn't pay me for two years, and I don't think she ever would have if I hadn't forced her."

"What did you do to force her?" asked Glory.

"Well, at the time I was collecting in a dump truck. I just drove in with a full load of very smelly garbage and told her that I was going to park in her driveway until I got what was coming to me. She paid up right then for the whole two years. And what's more she pays up regularly now.

"Of course most people are decent enough," continued Gore, and Sue could see that he enjoyed explaining his business to Glory. "The trouble is that they all get talked out of their money by everybody else, and there isn't anything left to pay the trashman with. You see, we're all classified as 'consumers,' and that means 'purchasing fools.' The only way the economy can be kept going properly is for everybody to buy, and then buy some more. People like Bill, here, and myself, we don't work enough to make money enough to spend enough, so we're some kind of economic outlaws. We're not even in debt like most everybody else. In fact, if we could collect from all of the people who moved away without paying their trash bill we could have ourselves a pretty good fling."

"Do you own this land?" Glory asked.

"Sure," Gore told her. "I own ten acres here, but of course it's cheap land. It wasn't worth much when I bought it, and now that I've got a junkyard on it, it's worth even less. Bill owns his trailer and I'd give him the land it's on only he says he doesn't care. Fred's shack is on my property too, but that doesn't bother me. What are brothers good for if they can't share, especially when they don't have much anyway.

"But you're right about warning Jack," Gore concluded. "He's got to finish his high-schooling so that if he doesn't *want* to be in the trash and junk business he won't *have* to. Actually, it doesn't hurt to be smart when you run a junkyard, you know. You have to have a special kind of memory so that you can remember where each old wreck is and what parts you've sold off it and what parts are left and how much they're worth."

There was the sound of a car driving into the yard, and Gore rose to look out the window. "Pardon me," he said, "I've got a customer."

He went out. Glory followed at a distance, and Sue stayed at the doorway to watch and to listen.

The car was a rather ancient Oldsmobile, and the driver, remaining at the wheel and talking to Gore through the rolled-down window, seemed to be a reasonably well-dressed middle-aged man. He had metal-rimmed glasses and a somewhat puffy red face.

"You buy second-hand cars, don't you?" he asked Gore as he turned off the key.

"No, I buy junk," Gore told him, adding, "and I pay junk prices."

"Oh, I know," said the man with a smile, "but this car is quite old and a second-hand dealer wouldn't be interested in it. I figured that since you can resell the engine you would be able to pay a reasonable price. The car is worn, but as you can see, it is running perfectly."

59

"Ten dollars is my price for junk cars," Gore said. "I can't afford second-hand car prices because that's not my business."

"But an engine that is in such fine condition, running so smoothly," protested the man.

"Well, start her up again and I'll give a listen," Gore said.

"All right," said the man, "and notice how easily it starts."

The engine did start instantly, and it ran smoothly. Gore kept his usual buying-face, which means that he did not show that he was pleased or even interested. He opened up the hood and watched the whirrings and listened to the buzzings and clickings inside. He took a screwdriver out of his pocket, touched it to the top of the engine and then put his ear against the handle, as if he were a doctor sounding the heart of his patient. Then he went around the car to the other side and continued his close inspection. Glory went around with him, looking over his shoulder, an intern studying the doctor's methods of diagnosis.

"Race it," called Gore.

The engine speeded up to a light roar and then quieted.

"More, and faster," said Gore.

Again the engine raced, but it seemed as if the driver were holding back from top speed. Still showing no sign as to whether he liked or disliked the car, Gore closed the hood.

Another car turned into the yard, new and gleaming in red magnificence, a woman at the wheel.

"That's my wife," said the man. "She came to give me a ride home if you buy the car. What do you think of that engine? Runs beautifully, doesn't it?"

Gore said, "I suggest that you drive it to a second-hand car lot and tell them about it." He turned to walk away.

"Wait!" called the man. "Don't you think that it's worth something. How about thirty-five dollars?"

"What's the matter?" asked Gore. "Don't you dare drive it down the road?"

"Of course I do," sputtered the would-be salesman indignantly. "You heard how easily it started and how smoothly it ran."

"Then go ahead," said Gore, "and drive it down the road. I only pay ten dollars for junk cars, and an engine with a cracked block is junk."

"Oh," said the man, apparently very surprised. "I didn't know it had a cracked block. I thought the engine was in perfect condition. I certainly wouldn't try to mislead anyone. Well, if that's the case I'll take the ten dollars."

Without comment Gore reached into his back overalls pocket, withdrew a wad of money, and handed the man a ten-dollar bill. Stuffing it rather hastily into his wallet, the man retreated to the other vehicle, where his plump, unsmiling wife sat sternly at the wheel. She immediately backed the car out of the yard, and the gleaming red chariot carried them away.

"A cracked block makes an engine worthless, doesn't it?" asked Glory, gazing after the departing couple.

"Sure does," Gore told her. "You probably couldn't drive this wreck two miles back to town before it would run out of water, and probably oil too."

"And he knew it too, didn't he?" she demanded.

"Look, it's just a game some people like to play," said Gore, holding the door of the trailer open for her. "It's like old-fashioned horse trading. A junkman is an easy target. Try to beat him at his own game—sell him junk at the going price of good stuff. People try it all the time. Once in a while someone will come in with a hunk of iron and tell me it's an antique. They think that since I'm a junkman I must be stupid, so they figure it'll be easy to put one over on me. I had a friend who went broke and lost his junkyard because he got fooled so many times."

Bill had started supper while Gore had conducted the business transaction. So Glory stayed and ate with them, to Sue's delight. Gore returned to his house to take care of poor Fred, whom everyone had forgotten in the excitement of the hour.

In the trailer the talk turned to horses, and Sue was able to spin Glory along for hours by questioning her about horses she had owned as a child. Glory spoke so well she could make the Kentucky countryside come alive as she talked of the rolling blue-green fields, the

62

white board fences, and the chestnuts and bays and blacks she had known and ridden in her childhood. She told of horse shows she had entered, and of horseback camping trips, jumping contests and races, and of falls she had taken.

When Glory left, Sue went straight to her homework, but her mind just wouldn't stay with her English grammar. She was jumping Houri over white board fences and then wondering how a life of such pleasure could be real and not evaporate the way her dreams did.

9.

Fred Servey improved in the next few days and was able to work at his new job the following Monday. That night a letter arrived from his wife saying that she needed him and the children needed him, much more than they all needed money. The family wanted to come and live with him, no matter how small his shack and no matter how little money they would have to live on.

"I guess we never knew how much you meant to us all until you went away," she wrote. "Now we've tried, and we know we can't live without you. Please

64

come and get us and take us out of this place and back to the country as soon as you can."

Fred wept as he read the letter over and over, and he wept as he gave it to Sue and asked her to read parts of it aloud to the others.

"We'll have to clean out your place," said Bill. "We must have three or four tons of scrap iron stored in it."

"They need me," Fred repeated for the third or fourth time. "Nan needs me and the children need me. I wish I could go right down there tonight and get them."

"I'd let you use my car," offered Bill, "but I don't think that the old wreck is safe to make the trip in. You'd be almost sure to break down somewhere on the high way."

"If you go on a Sunday and come back the next day you can use the trash truck," said Gore. "It's in pretty good shape and there'll be plenty of room to put everybody's things in. The only trouble would be if it rains, but you can string a canvass across part of it. That way you can bring back some furniture too."

"I doubt if there's any left. Well, I can't go for at least two weeks. I'll write her tonight and explain that I just got this job and that I'll have to wait for a couple of paychecks." Fred looked around the room at them. "You just don't know what this means to me. Why, I've been worrying about my family day and night for two months now. I've hardly dared to think of what's happening to them. And now they need me and they want to live in the house I built for them."

Suddenly his face brightened. "You know, if I could paint that shack it really wouldn't look too bad. I put it together in a nice spot there on the side of the hill with that big maple tree in front of it."

"I've got some paint," offered Gore. "There's four gallons of white paint that somebody threw out in their trash last fall. I saved it out because it's perfectly good. They were just too lazy to stir it. You can have it if you want. I've got a few other shades in smaller cans too. Let's go and look right now."

The two left, and Sue, again studying English grammar, found it difficult to concentrate. She thought that both the new job and the fact that his family needed him might combine to reverse Uncle Fred's run of bad luck. He had seemed like a different person, a new man, because of the letter. And, though he had been satisfied to have the shack unpainted for months, suddenly he cared enough to paint it and make it look nice.

Sue forced her thoughts back to homework. She finished correcting sentences for English and then looked at her assignment book to find out what she had left to do. She noted with disgust that there was homework in a subject that was almost always free of such a disagreeable task—home economics. This seemed the last straw. There was a pamphlet to read concerning the county contest in homemaking. The teacher had given instructions that everyone in the class must enter a project. Sue had never taken part in any contest before, and

66

she felt she had too much to do to bother with this one. She would much rather let the girls who were good at sewing and cooking enter their projects, while she spent her time with the chestnut mare. She couldn't see how the teacher could give a student a low mark for not entering, but she didn't dare challenge Miss McMurtrie's decision.

Sue was trying to think of an appropriate project that wouldn't take a lot of time, when the door flew open with a bang. Gore entered with Uncle Fred, who looked very strange, rather pale and glassy-eyed and gasping. He seemed to be dizzy, and Gore helped him to the sofa. For a moment Fred's face seemed to fill with despair, and he put his hands over his eyes.

Her father had half risen from his chair. "What happened?"

"I guess he wasn't ready to look at paint," said Gore. "We opened a can of that paint and as soon as he began stirring it he almost passed out. He was sick for a few minutes but he seems better now."

"How do you feel, Fred?" Bill asked.

"As if I'd been hit in the head and the stomach with a sock full of sand."

"Get him some aspirin, Bill," ordered Gore, and then asked Fred, "Do you think we should get the doctor?"

"No, I'm okay now, or I will be after I get those aspirins. I guess I'd better give up the idea of painting my shack, though. I'll have to stay away from paint for a while."

The words came from Sue almost before she had thought of saying them. "Let me paint it, Uncle Fred. I can do it in my spare time, and it will be my homecoming gift to your family."

Fred had tossed two aspirins into his mouth and was just taking a drink of water to wash them down. He coughed and nearly choked.

"You?" he sputtered. "A girl paint? Why you'd have to get up on a ladder to do that!"

"Well, is there any reason why a girl should *not* get up on a ladder?"

"I wouldn't throw away a good offer if I were you," her father told him. "I can help Sue get started tomorrow afternoon. It's not a big building and it isn't high. I bet she'll do just as good a job as any one of us."

Sue realized that this was an exaggeration and that everyone knew it, but she appreciated it anyway. She was a bit irritated at Fred's reaction. It didn't seem quite the way to respond to an offer of help.

Jack said, "Sure, Uncle Fred. Sue can do some of it anyway, and I'll empty all the junk and scrap we've been storing in there."

"Well, I sure do appreciate your offer," Fred told Sue. "I'm just not used to having girls offer to do jobs like that. It would be wonderful to have that place painted when Nan first sees it. She might even like if it was pretty to look at. And I guess I'm in no shape to do any painting."

"In fact," Gore said, "you'd better not go near

there once the painting has started. You can sleep at my place in the meantime."

"Well, I sure thank you all. You don't know what it means to have people offer to help when you're down and out. Now, Gore, if you'll just let me lean on your shoulder I'll get right to bed. I sure can't afford to be sick on my second day at work. I feel as if a good long sleep would put me back in shape."

Two nights later Sue had the front of the shack painted and was up on the short ladder, working on the side nearest the road. Glory, back from riding Houri and rubbing her down, was stretched out on the grass watching her and listening to the story of Uncle Fred and his reaction to the can of paint.

"Well, I think that this is a great idea," Glory told her, "but don't you neglect your riding. It's just like learning to play a musical instrument. You never get any good at it without a great deal of practice."

"I'll keep it up," promised Sue. "If I ride for an hour after I get home, I can paint until suppertime. Dad is going to have supper late so that I can get more done each day. If I paint on Saturday and Sunday morning I can get one coat done this week and at least half of another. After all, this is important too."

"Yes, I know," Glory agreed, "and I think that you're great to be doing it. I just don't want you to abandon this horse business right now. You're a natural on horseback, and you owe it to yourself to improve as fast as you can. Everybody needs to have something that they love to do and that they're really good at. With you it could be riding, at least for a few years."

"I'll try," Sue promised.

She painted several boards while Glory lay watching her in silence. At her next words Sue nearly dropped the paint bucket.

"What would you think of entering Houri in the Arlingham Horse Show?"

Sue regained her balance and stood on the ladder for a moment, the brush uplifted motionless, paint running down her arm and dripping off her elbow. She asked, facing the fresh-painted wall, watching a stuck fly struggling to get loose, "Did you say what would I think of entering Houri in the Arlingham Horse Show?"

"Why not?" asked Glory.

"Well, in the first place it's twenty-five miles from here . . ."

"I'll rent a horse trailer and pull it with my Jaguar."

"In the second place it costs money to enter each event in the show . . ."

"Less than you'd think. The fee really isn't much, and you wouldn't have to enter more than a couple of events. I can ride her in the hunter class and you can enter the walk, trot, canter, and the novice equitation classes."

"And in the third place," began Sue helplessly, feeling a bit like the fly stuck in the paint, "I don't ride well enough to . . ."

70

"You will by then if you work at it hard enough."

"And last . . ."

"I'm glad it's last."

"It comes in late June, a couple of weeks after you'll get out of college."

"I'm going to stay on at the college until the first of July. I'm working on a project with one of my professors and we won't be finished until then. The horse show is on a Saturday and won't interfere."

Sue dipped the brush into the bucket, wiped the excess on the rim, and painted a few strokes, needing something to do while her thoughts untangled.

"No more objections?" asked Glory.

"I don't have proper riding clothes."

"Blue jeans are all right. There aren't any requirements. You already have my old riding boots and we can take turns using my hardhat. There'll be other kids in make-do riding clothes. The best-dressed riders don't automatically win, you know."

There was a long pause. Glory lay back and gazed at the late afternoon sky. Sue moved another step down the ladder and painted a new board.

Glory asked, "Sue, do you really not want to go?"

"It . . . it's not that," Sue stammered. "It's just that I never dreamed of it and I can't get used to the idea. I can't imagine riding in the Arlingham Horse Show. I've only seen a horse show once in my life and it wasn't a very big one."

"And there's another thing . . ." she began.

"What is it, Sue?"

She came down the ladder and set the paint bucket on the ground. "Do you think . . . I mean, will Houri be all right? Well, do you think she knows how to be in a horse show?"

"Don't worry about Houri. I'll bet that mare knows her way around. And we'll train her to do the same things that she'll have to do there. My guess is that she's been in horse shows before. Now, shall we shake on it, Sue?"

"My hands are all paint, and besides, I have to see what Dad says."

"Okay, you talk to him and I will too. And this Saturday we'll begin practice along with the regular riding lesson. Now I'll go back to Bickner and leave you to your painting."

10.

Early June became the busiest period of time in Sue's twelve and a half years. Home from school at 3:30, she ran to the shed. Banging on the feed bucket into which she had thrown a handful of oats, she enticed Houri in from the pasture. The mare submitted willingly enough to being saddled and bridled, and she seemed to enjoy the hour of walking, trotting, cantering, turning, and backing, as horse and rider came to test each other's wills and respect each other's strengths.

Following this practice session came a fifteen-minute rubdown for the mare and a cleanup of tack. Then Sue changed into her "paint clothes," a pair of worn and tattered blue jeans already covered with flecks and smears of white paint. She painted for an hour and a half or so, and it always took so long to clean up afterward that she couldn't sit down to supper until seven.

Homework followed, and there was usually quite a lot of it. But there was one subject that Sue didn't worry about any more—home economics. The teacher had become quite insistent that every girl undertake a project similar to those called for by the state "Young Homemakers" contest. The teacher would choose the projects from the school that would be written up for the state competition. A local group of judges would then pick the best entry from the county.

The projects would take the place of all homework for the rest of the year and would count toward a grade for the final marking period. Sue had at first been resentful of having to do anything more than she had already undertaken. Then she hit upon the idea of asking if her house painting and decorating work could count as a project. When she was told that it could, she entered the contest, only to avoid having to do anything more. If *hours* counted she would certainly get a good mark, she thought. There would not be many other girls who would be putting in nearly two hours a day plus many more hours on weekends.

Bedtime brought with it the pleasure of knowing that the day had been well spent. There was a real feeling of self-improvement that came with her sessions on the

74

chestnut mare. Horse and rider were working more and more closely with each other. There was a kind of harmony that she felt, and she believed that Houri felt it too. She could not explain how it happened, even to herself, but it was as if Houri could more and more sense her will and wanted only to respond. The eager mare, her ears pricked forward, needed no pulling and tugging at the reins for direction, only a gentle urging, and she seemed to be almost as sensitive to pressure from the knees as she was to the hands.

And bedtime brought the added pleasure of relaxing muscles tired in a service of kindness and generosity. By Tuesday of the second week she had completed two coats on the outside of the shack, improving its looks immensely. Her father had helped her on Sunday, and Janet had worked with her on two afternoons. Everyone agreed that no miner's shack had ever been dressed so well. In fact, Gore had begun to refer to it as "The White House," and so it became to them all.

Fred told her at least once every morning and again every night how much he appreciated the job she was doing. He mowed a little patch of grass on the hillside above and below his house to make a lawn, and on Saturday he dug up a pair of wild azaleas and planted one on either side of the front door, and somehow the effect was immediate. The shack had become a home.

Sue did not pause in her work to watch the moving or the transplanting. When the outside was painted, she went to the hardware store in town and picked out a tan for the living room and bedroom woodwork and a light blue for the kitchen, paying for them with her own money. Of course she knew that no amount of paint could conceal the fact that this was really only a miner's shack, much too small for a family of eight, and she knew that both rooms would be used as bedrooms, but at least she would try to make it as attractive as possible.

She was glad when Fred found that his family could not be ready to leave the city quite as soon as they had expected, for this gave her another week in which to work. Fred had wired the building for electricity, so now that she was working inside, she began painting in the evenings. This meant that she had to get up early in the morning to do her homework.

Her father told her that he thought she was doing too much. She was getting dark circles under her eyes; she noticed it before he mentioned it. But he agreed on the importance of the task and upon the urgency of early completion. He painted the ceilings and agreed to help her wallpaper the living room. He figured out for her the number of rolls that she would need, and Gore agreed to pay for them, but neither man was willing to have any part in choosing the pattern, nor was Fred any help in making the decision. She discovered that the store would allow her to take home one of its catalogues, so that she could hold a sample on the wall against the tan woodwork. She knew that Glory could decide in a minute for her, but there was no time to wait to ask her. The salesman told her that the paper had to be ordered three days in advance, and it was Tuesday of the third week before she realized this. She called in Janet, and they agreed on a small print that was mostly yellow. Later Glory confirmed their choice, assuring them that she could have done no better.

Janet wanted to help, felt the excitement of preparing a home for a family. "It's like playing dollhouse, only it's real," she sighed. But her home-economics project, a dress made from her own pattern, of cloth she had dyed herself, was taking most of her time. The contest closed Friday and she had much left to do.

Sue had heard about some of the other students' projects. One girl was weaving cane seats in a set of old dining-room chairs, another had made a braided rug. A student whose father was an artist had made a set of clay bowls and cups and glazed them in her father's kiln. Most girls, like Janet, had made items of clothing. Sue had been a bit worried that the teacher might not accept her house painting and papering as a project, particularly as it was for another family, but that had not been a problem. Miss McMurtrie had been quite enthused about it.

On Wednesday after her ride, Glory came to make her twice-a-week tour of inspection of "The White House." Sue was busy trying to glue together an old rocking chair that Gore had saved from somebody's trash. Glory knelt beside her and put an arm over Sue's shoulder.

"Sue," she said, "I don't know what makes you tick. There's no woman on the place to tell you how to be feminine and do household things, yet you knew just what Fred and his family needed. And even though you've lived in a trailer next door to your Uncle Gore, who's never even fixed the hole in his porch floor nor the leak in his roof, you've done a wonderful job of changing a shack into a home that somebody can love. And all this while you're learning to ride like a cavalry officer. I just don't know how you do it."

"I guess I've been letting my schoolwork slide," said Sue, resisting an impulse to hug Glory with all her might for making her feel so noble. "My marks have gone down lately."

"Look, kid," Glory was kneeling with her beside the mending rocker, "marks aren't everything, and being smart with words doesn't make anybody so great. What's really important is the kind of person you are. It wouldn't make any difference to me whether you got high marks or low marks in school. You are somebody who can be counted on. You've got a big heart and you've got spirit. I don't ask for anything more in a friend."

This time Sue did hug her, although they nearly fell over in the process. She sighed, "I wish you were my sister, Glory."

"It's better to be friends," Glory smiled. "Sisters quarrel.

"And now," she said, changing her tone to appear businesslike, "you've got to cut me in on your enterprise here. I haven't done a thing to help, and I want to. What do you need that I can buy?"

"I was hoping to make curtains for the living room," Sue told her. "I think that Gore has some old curtain rods in the upper part of his storage shelter. I looked but I haven't found them yet. I priced some material in the store but I didn't think I could afford enough of it."

"Let's go right now," Glory said. "If we hurry we can get to the store before closing time."

Except for the day that Houri escaped, this was Sue's first ride in the Jaguar, yet her pleasure was not so much in the powerful growl of the engine, nor the swerve and polish of the car. It was riding with the top down beside Glory, blond hair whipping back from her exciting face, and it was having people in town turn and stare at them as they drove down Main Street.

At the store Sue explained, "This is the material I picked out, but you may like something different."

Glory spent several minutes looking at all of the available fabrics and then said, "I would have picked the same one, I think. Give me that scrap of paper you've got the window measurements on. We may as well get something for the kitchen too. Will this white chinz be okay? And get curtain rods. They don't cost much, and you may never find the ones that Gore thinks he has in his shelter."

Glory argued her into going into the drugstore for a soda on the way home. Sue, who ordinarily would rather die than be seen in town with paint-covered blue jeans, somehow felt that sitting at the counter beside Glory made the paint a matter of no importance.

Later, at home, her father promised to help her the next evening with wallpapering. He had borrowed

79

some tools for the job, and if the paper arrived at the store in time, Sue was to bring it home, cut her riding practice short by a few minutes, and then prepare an early supper so that they would have a long evening and could do the entire job in one session.

The paper did arrive. Father and daughter began the job early in the evening while Jack stayed in the trailer and washed the dishes.

Wallpapering proved to be a difficult and frustrating task. The paper stuck to itself and to Sue when she tried to pick it up. It was difficult to match the pattern, and cutting the top and bottom straight seemed almost impossible at first. But as the two of them began to get the feel of it they developed techniques, and a kind of ease and smoothness came into their work. The little area over and under windows still presented a problem, but floor-to-ceiling pieces went on easily. They worked silently most of the time—Sue covering the pieces with paste and holding them up to the wall, Bill lining up the pattern, cutting, and trimming.

Wallpapering can't be rushed, and it was 10:30 that night before they finished. Bill told Sue to go to bed while he cleaned the floor and table of scraps of paper and gobs of paste. It wasn't until she crawled into bed that Sue realized that she hadn't even looked around the room at the finished job. She remembered for one fleeting instant that she must rise early and do her homework, and then she fell asleep.

In the morning, at a quarter to six, her alarm went off and she lay struggling for consciousness until she remembered "The White House." She threw back the covers, jumped out of bed, washed, dressed, and ran out the door, across the field and up the little hillside. She burst into the newly decorated room, and it was a wonder to her eyes. All the little rips and jagged cuts and bumps which she had worried about last night melted away. The room was lovely. The patterned, yellow paper transformed it into a place of beauty and delight.

On an impulse she ran back to the trailer and collected her homework—books, paper, pen and pencil, and a blanket. Returning to the room, she spread the blanket on the newly-swept floor. She decided that for this hour and a half she would reap the reward for her hours of work. For this short time the room—indeed the entire house—was hers.

11.

Late that afternoon she was again in the "White House," sewing the last of the living room curtains. The other three were already up on the new rods and they matched very well the new paper and the tan woodwork.

She was startled by a knock on the door. Somehow, the thought of anyone knocking on the door of this empty house had never occurred to her, but there it was again. She rose from the mended rocking chair, walked to the door, and slowly, almost fearfully, opened it.

There, to her astonishment, stood her home economics teacher.

"Why . . . Why come in, Miss McMurtrie," she gasped, trying not to let the shock be too apparent.

"Hello, Sue," the teacher said, smiling. "Do you know why I've come to call on you?"

"Why . . . Well, no. I mean yes," said Sue confused. "I guess you want to investigate my home economics project to be sure I really did it." That didn't sound right after she had said it, so she added, desperately hoping that she could say *something* right, "It's nice of you to come. This is what I've been doing—painting, mostly. My dad helped me with wallpapering last night."

Miss McMurtrie looked around the house. "I entered your project in the state homemaking contest," she said. "It is one of three entries from our school. These will be judged with others from this county and the winner will be judged with others around the state from other counties. I entered yours on the basis of what you had written about it. Now that I see what you've done, I know that I made the right choice."

"Oh, but, Miss McMurtrie," Sue cried in horror. "I wasn't expecting to enter this in the state contest. I just wanted to get credit in home ec class so that I wouldn't have to take time to do a real project like making clothes. You see, I do riding practice with my horse every afternoon as soon as I get home from school, and then I work on this place. I painted the outside and the inside and fixed this chair and helped with the wallpaper and sewed the curtains. I only called this my project so that I could get as much time as possible to work on it. I thought that I was lucky when you didn't mind my using it. If you had said no I would have had to take time off from this job to make something for class. I even had to do all of my homework early this morning because my dad and I worked here so late last night."

"Your friend Janet has been telling me about what you have been doing here," said Miss McMurtrie. "She said that she thought it should be entered in the state contest, so that's two of us, even if you don't think so."

"Oh, but, Miss McMurtrie, there wasn't much sewing, just these curtains. And I didn't do any of this to try to win a prize. I was only helping out. You see, my Uncle Fred gets sick from paint fumes so he couldn't do the work. And the men didn't want to choose the decorations so I did that."

"Did you pick out the wallpaper, Sue? It's a lovely pattern and it goes well with the woodwork."

"Janet helped me, or that is, we both looked through the catalogue and then agreed on this paper."

"It's a very good choice. And what about the curtains? They go well with everything, and they make this living room a very pleasant place."

"Well," Sue began, delighted that someone appreciated her selections, "I picked out the material but I couldn't afford it. Then my friend Glory who gives me riding lessons wanted to help, so she bought the cloth and the rods. And she picked out this white material for the kitchen windows."

"Sue, you've been working very hard at this for quite a while, haven't you?" Miss McMurtrie asked, a tone of admiration in her voice.

"About three weeks," Sue answered. "You see, Uncle Fred built this place last fall for his family to live in. Then they didn't want to come here because his wife didn't want to live in a miner's shack anymore. She had spent her whole life in miners' shacks and she had hoped that they could get a better home.

"So they moved to the city. Uncle Fred couldn't get work there and he came back here. Now his family wants to come and live with him, and he has a job. He's going to the city to get them tomorrow and bring them back Sunday. I just want to have the house look nice so that his wife will like it when she comes here."

Miss McMurtrie was trying to write something on a piece of paper. She began to sit down on a chair that Sue had been fixing.

"Oh, not there, Miss McMurtrie," Sue gasped, just in time. "I haven't finished gluing that chair yet. The rocker is all right, though. You see, these were old chairs that my Uncle Gore saved out of the trash. He saves a lot of things that he thinks he might use sometime. Usually we can't find them when we want them, though."

Miss McMurtrie continued writing. She said, "Sue, I am jotting down some comments to send along with your entry blank for the state contest. I want to see that you get recognition for this work. It is one of the most impressive things I've ever seen a youngster do. You have not only worked harder and longer than anyone else, I'm sure of that, but you have done it entirely out of kindness. You have had nothing to gain for yourself. In fact, Janet told me that you've never even seen your aunt and her children."

"No, I haven't," said Sue, "but I did it for Uncle Fred, too. He's had an awful lot of bad luck, but recently it changed and he's started having good things happen, like getting this job and having his family tell him they need him. So I thought that I'd help to keep his good luck coming by making sure that his family stayed after they got here. That's why I got started, but after I got going I sort of liked it. As Janet says, it's like playing dollhouse only it's real."

"Well, it's not only a kind thing to do, Sue. You have done a very fine job here. I'm really proud of your choice of decorations. You have shown very good taste."

"Now just sign the application on this line," she said, pointing and handing her pen to Sue, "and let's call your project 'Decorating a Home.' I'll take this back to school with me. The judges are meeting very soon and I want to have this ready for them."

"I wish you'd tell them that I didn't do it just to win a prize," said Sue. "I wasn't even thinking of getting any attention for it."

"I have mentioned that in my comments," Miss McMurtrie said reassuringly. "I think that's an important part of your project."

86

She went out the door just as Bill Servey was coming up from the trailer.

"This is my father," Sue said. "Dad, this is Miss McMurtrie, my home economics teacher."

Miss McMurtrie explained her plan to enter Sue's project in the state home economics contest. Bill thought that it was a fine idea.

"You have a very hard-working daughter, Mr. Servey," she said as she got into her car.

"We're all proud of her," said Bill. "She's been the only woman on the place for quite a spell now, and she does right well."

Miss McMurtrie backed her car out of the narrow driveway and waved at them as she drove off.

Sue told her father, "You know I didn't even think of doing this just to try to win a prize. She decided that, and I guess Janet suggested it to her. Wait until I see Janet!"

"Well, Sue," he said, putting his arm around her shoulders as they walked along to the trailer, "I'm glad it worked out this way. Don't get your heart set on a prize, but if you get one, you'll deserve it."

About eight thirty that evening a car drove in while Sue was hanging the last of the kitchen curtains. She heard voices and went to the door. It was Miss McMurtrie again, this time with two women and a very tall straight man whom she recognized as Mr. Patterson, the superintendent of schools.

"I'm back again, Sue," said Miss McMurtrie, "and

I've brought the judges who will decide which project will win for our county. All of the entries except yours and one other could be judged at the school. We already have been to see Frances Breen's herb garden and I wanted to be sure they had an opportunity to see your project. I thought that you would be working tonight, and I see I am right."

She introduced the judges: Miss Thayer, who owned a dress shop in town; Mrs. Miller, who was the dietician at the hospital; and Mr. Patterson.

Miss McMurtrie and the two ladies went in while Mr. Patterson looked at the outside of the house. When he came in a few minutes later he asked, "Did you paint the outside too? It looks like it has had two coats."

"My dad helped me," Sue explained. "My Uncle Fred can't paint because he gets sick from the fumes, and Uncle Gore has a hard time painting because he has only one arm. But Gore got the paint for the outside. It was some that somebody threw away because it was all hard in the bottom. We used an old egg beater to stir it up."

"Her father and uncle have a trash route," explained Miss McMurtrie, and it was the first time Sue had ever heard anyone say that without feeling that there was a slightly insulting tone behind it.

"My dad painted the ceilings too," Sue said. "He told me that they were too hard for me. I bought all the inside paint myself with my allowance money that Dad gives me."

The judges asked her more questions about the project, mostly the same ones that Miss McMurtrie had asked. They seemed impressed by her work, she thought.

"I know this has nothing to do with your project, Sue," Mr. Patterson said, "but I don't see how a family with six children can live in a house of this size. There is only one bedroom, and the living room isn't very large. Where will everyone fit?"

Miss Thayer told him, "Plenty of poor people with big families live in places like this or even smaller. It isn't easy, but they all find a place to lie down at night, even if it's only on a blanket on the floor."

Mr. Patterson shook his head. "Well, it may be small, but you've certainly done an excellent job of fixing it up, Sue."

The judges said good-bye and left.

Sue decided that she had done enough for the night, so she shut off the light and went home. She wondered what the judges thought of her project. She found herself hoping that she might win a prize.

On Sunday Sue and Glory were so involved in their riding lesson that they didn't notice the young man approaching until he called to them from the pasture fence.

"Are you Susan Servey?" The man was college age and very fat. He had short black hair and black hornrimmed glasses with thick lenses. Although it was a hot June day he wore a dark suit, the buttons of which were straining to hold him inside.

He was looking at Glory, and Sue laughed to think that he had mistaken the strikingly beautiful Bickner College student for herself. Still it was a bit frightening to have this stranger calling her name. As she trotted Houri up to the fence she studied the large black bag that the man had slung over his shoulder. She decided that it was a camera bag and that he was a newspaper reporter. She allowed herself the luxury of a proud thought—her project had won a prize. She had decided last night that compared to many of the girls' projects perhaps hers might be considered a good one. The reporter now must have been sent to write about it. She tried to remember what second and third prizes were.

"You the Servey girl?"

"Yes."

"I'm John Bottomly with the *Valley Transcript* and I've got to do a story on you and the project that won the prize. Want to get a picture of you but you'll have to get off that horse."

"What prize did I win?"

"You mean they didn't notify you from school?"

"We don't have a phone."

"Well, I'll be darned! Then let me be the first to congratulate you. You won first prize in the county contest, so you're fifteen dollars richer. How does that make you feel? Hey wait! I haven't got all day!"

The word "first" had passed like an electric shock through her. She had allowed herself to think that it was possible, but had not dared believe it. Now she still felt the shock, but it went in rapid stages from satisfaction to pride to joy. She swung the mare around and cantered back to Glory.

90

"First prize!" she called. "I won first prize for the whole county!"

"They must have had a good panel of judges," Glory said calmly. "Usually I disagree with judges' choices, but this time the right person won."

"There were a lot of good projects," Sue told her. "I was lucky."

"You're just lucky that they had good judges. Now go and give the man your story. I'll ride Houri until you get back."

"Do I have to tell him everything?" asked Sue.

"It's better to answer his questions so that he gets it right instead of letting him make it up, the way some reporters do."

At the "White House" the reporter photographed her on the steps. Then they went inside and he took out a pad of paper on which to write notes as he asked her about the project. To Sue's horror he sat down heavily in one of the chairs that she had not finished mending.

The collapse was gradual and colossal. The chair, complaining with several weary and surprised creaks, simply sagged to one side while the overweight young man frantically tried to raise himself with his arms extended in front of him as if grabbing for an invisible rope. As the chair completely abandoned itself to the breakdown, the creaks changed to splintering snaps and with a final crash deposited its seat, unbroken and still containing the alarmed Mr. Bottomly rather rudely on the floor. The young man sat in the rubble blinking for a moment and Sue, having thrown her hands over her face in dismay, peeked out between her fingers and although she tried, could not say anything. She watched as he separated himself from the wreckage, rolling over on his knees and then rising, dusting his trousers, and then stooping to pick up his writing pad.

"Are you all right?" Sue finally managed.

"Yes," sighed Mr. Bottomly and then added what seemed like an unnecessary statement, "I guess I've ruined your chair."

Sue lowered her hands from her face and murmured, "I hadn't glued that one together yet." She added, trying to get things back to normal, "The rocking chair will hold you all right," then wondered if it had been the right thing to say.

The interview continued after he had rather cautiously lowered his bulk into the rocking chair, which moaned the tiniest bit but held. Sue explained the problems of her Uncle Fred and his family while Mr. Bottomly scribbled unrecognizable notes on his pad.

Afterward he prepared to take another picture of her. This time she was to pose as if she were just putting up a curtain in the living room.

"Now let's have a nice big smile," he told her, but she was much too self-conscious to manage one.

He moved about the room trying to find the best camera angle, and as he did Sue looked at the wreck of the chair and began to think of how funny he had looked, clutching frantically at the air as he went down. She nearly laughed out loud at the thought, and at that moment there was a blinding flash and she realized the picture had been taken.

Mr. Bottomly thanked her for the story and left. Sue watched him drive out of the yard, and then she raced to the pasture, where Glory was standing by the chestnut mare, adjusting the girth.

"Are you going to be in the headlines?" she asked.

"Well, I didn't ask him what he is going to do with the story," Sue said, and then she realized that Glory was joking.

"Just as long as you looked glamorous when he took your picture it will be all right. I'll be looking for it on the family page."

"I couldn't smile no matter how hard I tried until I remembered what he looked like when the chair collapsed," Sue told her, "and then I had all I could do to keep from laughing."

She began to tell Glory about Mr. Bottomly's descent, but the more she told the more she began to smile and then giggle, so that by the time she had finished, the two of them were so weak from laughter that they were holding onto each other for support and the tears were streaming down their cheeks.

Sue spent most of the afternoon cleaning the little house—washing the windows, picking up the tools and scraps, including the result of Mr. Bottomly's catastrophe, and sweeping and mopping the floor. She tidied up the few items of furniture and then surveyed the room. It was rather bare, but she thought that it really did look quite nice.

For a moment she wished that the reporter could take a picture of her project in its final form, and then she decided that her work was not for the public, not for the prize money, in fact perhaps not even for Fred Servey and his family. She must be content with her own pride in the accomplishment, her own satisfaction of a job well done. When her father came in to announce that it was suppertime he stood beside her surveying the living room. She had placed a large vase of wildflowers on the table and it seemed to add just the right touch needed to make the room attractive. Bill put his arm over her shoulder and drew her to him. "I don't know what makes you the way you are, Sue," he said, "but whatever it is I like it."

Fred Servey and his family arrived late Sunday night long after Sue had gone to bed. She saw the truck in the driveway when she went to school the next morning. In the afternoon she went to call at the house and meet Mrs. Servey. She knocked at the door and thought that she heard someone shout for her to come in.

What she found was utter bedlam. There were children everywhere of all ages. A girl of perhaps nine sat in the rocking chair holding a screaming baby and trying to feed it from a bottle. A little boy with a dirty face and a runny nose ran naked around the room kicking pots and pans and boxes which were scattered everywhere, shouting all the while. A boy perhaps two years of age lay sound asleep on a blanket on the floor in the corner, sucking his thumb peacefully, unaware of the din around him. Another boy who Sue thought must be about seven was playing with a truck near the bedroom doorway making engine sounds at the top of his voice. Nan Servey and a girl slightly younger than Sue were washing clothes in a tub which was on the table where the flowers had been. Through it all the radio was turned to top pitch blaring out hillbilly music.

Mrs. Servey looked up at Sue as she entered. She nodded and Sue said hello. The woman went back to her washing. Her oldest daughter glanced up at Sue from time to time but kept at her work. There was no point in trying to carry on a conversation amid the deafening din, and no one offered to turn down the radio.

Sue stood a few moments trying to gather her thoughts together, found it hopeless, and left. She could not hold back a bitter tear of disappointment as she made her way slowly through the junkyard and up toward the pasture. She felt certain that the family she had found in her "White House" would have been just as well off if she had never even touched the miner's shack that was their home.

Later in the evening she told her father how she felt about this. His answer was, "Sue, winning that prize and getting a newspaper article done about yourself spoiled you. In the beginning you were doing that job because you wanted to. Then people told you how nice it all was, and they were right. This afternoon you went over there to collect that family's thanks just as if you were the landlord coming after the rent."

She started to protest but he held up his hand.

95

"I know you didn't think of it that way even though that's what it amounted to. But you see Nan is so bogged down with her own misery she can't even think of anything but how she's going to live through the day. After she settles down and the kids get used to the place, she will probably begin to enjoy life. But you can't expect her to be very gracious in the meantime."

Sue's story was in the newspaper the next night. The pictures, especially the smiling one, came out well. Mr. Bottomly's article contained a few mistakes, but she forgave him because she realized that he had been upset after his disaster with the chair. After all, she felt, there was no need to quibble over such fine points as whether the uncle that was going to live in the house was Fred or Gore.

The next day nearly everyone in school told her that they had seen her picture in the paper, and her teacher placed it on the bulletin board. Janet congratulated her several times, Glory came for her ride that night and was delighted with the picture.

It was a very pleasant experience to bask in the light of recognition but she had learned that you must never expect to collect gratitude as if it were owed to you.

12.

The Saturday lessons during the first two weeks of June became intense practice sessions. Under Glory's careful guidance and through her own nightly workouts, Sue had become a reasonably good rider. She had been on the highway with Houri many times by herself and had even tried the low jumps on a few occasions. Most important of all, she felt at ease on Houri's back. She rode with confidence, in command of a horse attentive to her every move.

She no longer dreaded the Arlingham Horse

97

Show. Rather, she looked forward to it. After school had closed for the summer, there would be only one Saturday for a lesson, but she could practice for long periods every day.

The last day of school arrived. Sue's report card was not all that it might have been, but she was presented with her prize of fifteen dollars at the school's final assembly and that honor partly made up for the low academic showing.

And through the last week before the show she rode in the cool of morning and evening every day, feeling the improvement, knowing at the end of the week that she was a better rider than she had been at the beginning. Still she lacked confidence, because she had never seen others of her age ride. The only person she knew who rode was Glory, who was older and an advanced horsewoman.

"Glory," she asked on that final afternoon, "do you really think it makes sense for me to ride in that horse show? I'm just so afraid that when I do badly people will ask why I thought I was good enough to enter in the first place."

"If you're going to be terribly disappointed when you don't take all the first prizes, then you'd better stay home."

"Oh, no! It's not that!" Sue insisted. "I just don't want to be the worst one in the ring. Everyone will notice."

Glory heaved an impatient sigh, took a breath, and began. "Sue Servey, I've told you this before in different ways, and I'll probably have to again, but here it is. There are style riders who know all of the proper terms and positions and who can go through all of the right figures but who just don't relate to the horse.

"And there are what I call joy riders. They're people who are kind of natural with a horse. A person like that usually has a strong will, and the horse senses it and becomes eager and alert. But without some kind of lessons or discipline such a person is usually a sky rider and an elbow flopper and all the other things that are okay until he has to compete against an accomplished horseman.

"Now you don't have enough experience for anybody to be sure yet how you'll turn out, but you're the third kind of rider, the natural with style."

"Everything you've done, Sue, I've made you do right. Your position is always right, but it's never stiff, always comfortable. You give the right commands and you remember how you're supposed to do everything. But more than that. When you're up on that chestnut mare, she not only knows you're in control—she's eager to find out what you want her to do.

"Houri becomes alert when you're on her. Anybody looking at you and that mare knows you're a team. She's more horse and you're more girl when you're together. It's a beautiful thing to see, Sue, and I'll bet that you can feel it when you're riding her even though you may not understand it. You do feel it, don't you?"

"Yes," she sighed, smiling dreamily.

"Then stop worrying. You're inexperienced and

that's going to show. Houri may act up, with a whole lot of other horses in the ring. She'll be tense and so will you, and you'll feel it in each other. That's why you shouldn't count on doing very well. But don't worry. Other people will be new too, and they'll be just as worried as you will. The more relaxed you can be, the more you try to have fun, and the more you worry about the chestnut mare instead of yourself, the better you'll do. I told you before, I wanted you in this because I think it would be good for you. If I had the least idea that you were going to do badly I wouldn't be arguing you into entering."

13.

The day of the show dawned hot and muggy. Sue was up almost as early as the sun, for she couldn't sleep. Besides they would need an early start. Houri must be loaded no later than eight, for it was an hour-and-a-half's drive to the Arlingham fairgrounds and the show opened at ten.

By the time Glory arrived at seven fifteen, Sue had been out to the shed four times, fed Houri, groomed her twice, swept the shed floor, wiped off the saddle and bridle. Bill didn't have breakfast quite ready but Glory helped him organize the little kitchen and soon, with Jack joining them, they sat down to the table.

"You sure she has all she needs to enter this?" Bill asked. "I always thought that you had to have a whole lot of money to get into a horse show."

"All she needs is a horse," Glory told him, "and a dollar fee for each class she enters. She's entering two and she has her two dollars buttoned in her shirt pocket, don't you, Sue?"

"Well, here's another fifty cents, Sue," Bill said, sliding it across the shiny tabletop. "You can get some lunch with it."

"Thanks, Dad, and don't worry. Houri will get me by today."

"Trailer throws your Jaguar some, doesn't it?" asked Jack between mouthfuls of pancake.

"Not bad," Glory told him. "As long as I take it slow I'll be all right."

"It'll be uneasy with the horse in it," Jack insisted.

"Time will tell," Glory said, for no other reason than to have the last word, but Jack was deep in another forkful of pancakes anyway.

She glanced at her watch. "Time to load up."

"Need any help?" Bill offered.

"Don't think so—we'll try and see. Come on anyway."

Jack, concentrating on his morning energy intake, stayed at the table and as the others left was last seen reaching for the remaining short stack of pancakes.

The trailer which Glory had rented was a small

and simple affair. The back gate was hinged at the bottom and opened down to make a loading ramp.

"Now we'll find out if Houri has ever been in one of these things," Glory said. "My notion is that this isn't her first horse show, but I could be wrong."

Sue led the mare out of her stall and handed the leadline to Glory, who walked up the ramp and into the trailer. Houri stopped at the ramp, put her ears forward, sniffed the ramp, stretched her neck out to inspect the mobile stall, tried the ramp with one foot as if she were testing its strength, then became tense and her hind legs began to shake.

Just when she thought Houri was going to back away, the mare sprang into the trailer, hardly touching the ramp and barely missing the roof with her head. Glory, sensing that this might happen, sprang out of the way. Bill swung up the ramp so that Houri could not change her mind, and Glory, after fastening the proper snaps, made her exit through the narrow door at the front of the trailer.

"She acted like she didn't trust that ramp but she wanted to go for a ride," Bill said.

They loaded saddle and bridle, curry combs, brush, hardhat, a bundle of hay, and the water bucket into the Jaguar, then Sue climbed in while Glory made one last check on all of the snaps and fittings and hitches.

"Be careful," said Bill to Sue.

"Don't worry about her," Glory assured him. "She's a good rider."

The Jaguar rolled through the yard at a much

more subdued speed than usual. Jack emerged from the trailer carrying his coffee cup, just in time to say, "So long," and wave, his fork still in his hand. As they swung onto the road, Sue turned and waved to her father, still standing by the shed. She suddenly thought he looked a little more stooped and old than she had noticed before, and he seemed kind of lonely as he watched them drive away. For no reason that she could understand her eyes filled with tears for just a moment.

Glory drove slowly, stopping twice along the way to be sure that Houri was in no difficulty in the trailer. They arrived in Arlingham at nine thirty and turned into the fairgrounds.

There was a scene of magnificent confusion at the parking lot. Trailers, cattle trucks, and every kind of homemade horse carrier surrounded an open space in which at least a dozen horses and riders were dodging each other, and those on foot were barely avoiding being trampled as they wandered back and forth on errands, business, chores, and visits.

The sound of snorts and neighs filled the air, and Houri joined the chorus in full voice.

Glory found a parking place but suggested they leave Houri in the trailer until it was nearly time for Sue's open trail class, which was second on the program. That would give them time to register and look around. With Glory leading the way and Sue dodging closely behind they twisted through the field of milling horses and people, past the men who were setting up the raffle booth and the women in aprons who were getting the food concession ready, down to the judges' stand to wait in line to register.

The constant scream of neighing horses, the stamping of hooves in trailers and trucks, the roar of motors as new trucks arrived, the pounding of the blacksmith, already at work, and the calls of riders, over the heads of the walkers—these were the sounds of the Arlingham Horse Show, and Sue was drawn into the excitement from the moment she arrived.

"Everyone seems to know everybody," she said uneasily into Glory's ear as they stood in line.

"Summer riding camps," she appraised, knowingly. "These kids learn riding at camp and then compete in shows all summer. They see each other at every show. There'd be more of them here if it wasn't so early in the season."

They finally worked their way to the clerk's desk and found that everything was in order. Sue was given a large round card with the number 53. Glory pinned it on the back of her shirt for her, and they went back to the trailer.

A voice rasped over the public address system ordering contestants for the lead-line class to proceed to the west ring.

"You've got about twenty-five minutes before your class begins," Glory said. "Probably the best thing to do now is to lead Houri around the area and let her get used to the excitement."

They let down the tailgate and backed her out of the trailer. Glory saddled her while Sue held her and did some last-minute brushing on her mane. Sue then led her slowly and aimlessly through the crowd for several minutes, careful to keep far enough away from any flying heels that might chance to be aimed in their direction. Houri was alert and a bit nervous but did not shy or pull away, for which Sue was grateful.

On her third trip past the trailer she heard Glory call, "Mount up and walk her around some more. The more of this she gets used to the better."

She rode to where she could look down the hill to the rings. In the west ring mothers or fathers or older brothers or sisters were leading ponies around while very young children sat stiff and self-conscious in the saddle.

The other ring was set up as a jumping course and the contestants were being run individually. As she watched a black Arabian crashed through a gate, knocking rails in every direction. The rider lurched, nearly toppled, then grimly stayed on. She and her black continued their course, knocking off the top rail at each of the jumps. A fat attendant in overalls and undershirt ran heavily out to pick up the shambles and restore the jumps.

It came to Sue at that moment that she didn't have to worry as much about her form as she did about her nerve. It took courage to continue to jump after you and your horse had made such a mess of things.

"Open Trail Horse Class, please come down to the west ring, first call," announced the speaker. Sue felt a moment of panic while she searched for Glory, then saw her close by, smiling and reassuring.

"It'll be a big class," Glory told her. "They've included both western and hunter seats. Just give Houri a chance to look good but keep her in control. Try not to pass anyone on the course but if you do, pass on the inside. And above all, enjoy yourself—ride comfortably and not any stiffer than you have to.

"Now get down to the gate, and good luck!"

The ringmaster had not let anyone in yet, and a crowd of more than a dozen horses and riders surged in a tight mass at the entrance. Sue decided to avoid them and turned Houri in tight slow circles halfway down the hill until the gate opened and the congestion cleared.

In the ring, she found that she had only to follow the leader—walking next to the fence, counter-clockwise.

"Trot, please," came the singsong call of the ringmaster and, with the slightest urging Houri broke into the familiar motion. So far not a hitch. Sue noted with gratitude that her mare seemed to have sense enough not to run into the horse ahead of her. A red-haired girl on a tall gray went by at a canter, yanking the reins furiously. On the other side of the ring someone's mount reared twice, then cantered sideways.

"Keep your eyes ahead, don't stare all over the place," hissed a voice below her at the rail. She turned to find Glory, then caught herself and concentrated on the shoulders of the rider ahead. She heard a horse close behind her and resisted the temptation to turn around.

"Walk, please," called the loud-speaker, then, "Canter."

The slightest prod with her heels sent Houri into an easy lope. Ahead the shoulders she had been watching lifted high on a rearing mount then tumbled, and the riderless horse broke into the center of the ring. Sue had no time to watch, reining Houri up short. On the ground a frightened face stared up almost underneath her. Sue held Houri still and thanked God that the mare obeyed, while horses piled up behind, bumping into each other, some charging around the crowd. Helping hands pulled the fallen rider under the fence to safety. The ringmaster had called for a walk as soon as the girl had fallen, but it took time to slow some of the mounts.

The way cleared, he called again for a canter, and the horses began to spread themselves evenly around the ring. That experience past, Sue felt a surge of confidence and she began to enjoy herself. After all, nothing worse could happen, she reasoned. A change of direction, then more walking, trotting, and cantering—she was becoming familiar with the ring, with the special moves involved in conforming to the speed and pattern.

The order was given to line up on the far side of the ring, facing the officials' stand. Now the open-trail obstacle course was set up, three white poles laid out on the ground a short distance apart, and then a row of hay bales. The object was to step over the poles without stepping on them, then to jump the hay bales.

Sue was fifth in line. The first two horses went

through without a hitch. The third shied sideways at the poles, causing the rider to twist out of the saddle and end in an unhappy position with his arms around the horse's neck, looking like a monkey. The fourth stepped neatly between the poles, then just as it seemed about to sail over the hay bales gave two bucks and with a vicious kick broke one to bits, sending hay ten feet in the air.

With this as prelude, Sue moved forward with Houri, and without giving herself time to worry, directed her over the bars. She listened for the sound of hoof on wood, counted the steps, then knew she was over without touching. The hay was no problem, since she had been jumping bales and boxes for weeks. Houri sailed over lightly, then was easily guided to her place in line.

With varying degrees of success the other contestants guided their mounts through the course and resumed position. For a few minutes the judge worked at his score sheet then went down the line of horsemen, telling certain ones to move around the ring again. Sue was one of these, and vaguely wondered whether being chosen meant that you were good or bad. She shot a glance at Glory, saw a big grin on her face, and decided it was good.

For a long time they circled, the same routine as before—trot, canter, walk, reverse direction. First one, then another rider was eliminated by being sent to the center of the ring. Her heart sank as the judge motioned her into the center with them. She had known she would be eliminated, yet it was a disappointment. A girl on a dapple gray gelding was told to join them. The rest in the class continued to circle for another minute or so, then all were called in.

"First prize, winner of the blue, Jim Torle, on Western Daybreak," called the announcer.

Sue gasped as the boy beside her moved forward to receive the the ribbon.

"I thought we were the ones who were eliminated," Sue whispered to a girl whose horse kept prancing sideways toward her.

"Silly," the girl shot at her, then rode forward as her name was called for second prize.

"Third prize, Sue Servey, riding Houri," was the announcement. Sue felt a tingling sensation go down her spine. Her ears were hot and she knew that she was blushing. But automatically she brought Houri up to the ringmaster, who pinned a yellow ribbon on her bridle. He said in a low voice, "You handled her very nicely when the rider fell in front of you."

She knew enough to say, "Thank you," but beyond that she was still in a daze. She returned to the lineup, next to the girl who had won second prize, who said, "Still think you're eliminated?"

"No, but I'm surprised," Sue told her.

"The judges know what they're doing," said the girl, smiling. "Where are you from?"

"Pittsford," Sue answered, "what about you?"

"Philadelphia," said the girl. "Where's Pittsford?"

"A few miles south on Route Seven. Did you come to this show all of the way from Philadelphia?"

"I'm from Red Ridge riding camp," the girl said as they rode out of the ring. "You'll see lots of us here. We take in all the shows for miles around during the summer, and we get most of the prizes, too, you'll see."

Glory was at the trailer waiting, her face lit with pride. "Now are you worried about looking foolish, Sue Servey?"

"No," Sue was beaming, "but I sure was surprised!"

"I tell you, you're a natural," Glory said, holding Houri while Sue dismounted. "You worked her beautifully."

"She's some mare," murmured Sue, putting her arms around Houri's neck.

"Let's loosen the girth a little and walk her around for a while," Glory suggested. "My class doesn't take place for an hour."

The girl who had talked to Sue in the ring came over with some of her friends from the camp a little while later and they all introduced themselves. They suggested that Sue come with them to the concession stand, and she was grateful for the half-dollar her father had given her. The girls from the camp were not at all snobbish even though it was evidently a rather expensive and exclusive place. They seemed to feel that since Sue could obviously ride, she was all right.

Later, Glory entered in the Hunter Hack Class. She rode magnificently and took both jumps without a fault. There were several men in this class, however, and she ended up with third prize. Sue was as proud to see her golden-haired friend ride forward for the yellow ribbon as she was when she won her own.

There was a lunch break immediately afterward, and both of the young men who had won first and second prizes came to ask Glory if they could take her to lunch. Since there wasn't any place to go to eat, she suggested that they buy hot dogs and soda and bring it all back to the trailer. The girls from Red Ridge Camp brought sandwiches and joined them. Between the two sets of providers, Sue was well fed. She had never been with such a wild, happy crowd, and yet she had no trouble feeling that she belonged.

Sue's second class was to be similar to the first except that there would be more obstacles and the course involved dismounting and leading the horse over some of them. She was no longer nervous, in fact she looked forward eagerly to this event, but there was an ominous change of weather approaching. A dark cloud was covering half of the sky, and rumbles of thunder could be heard.

Just as Sue was to ride out to the ring the first of the wind struck. The roof was blown off the concession stand, and papers were whisked into the air. The second gust followed almost immediately and carried large drops of rain.

"Get Houri in the trailer, saddle and all," Glory ordered, breathless as the force of wind and rain beat on them. Luckily she had put the top up on the Jaguar and as soon as they had tipped up the tailgate they ducked inside.

The fairgrounds was again a scene of confusion. People and horses blurred together in a gray mist; children scurried for cover behind trees, against trucks, in cars, while drenched parents searched for them in all of the wrong places. Horses reared and fought as trainers tried to hurry them into trucks and trailers. A few riders, convinced that the shower would soon be over, remained on their mounts, shouting confusing cries to each other. Expensive saddles, blankets, bridles, riding boots, were thrown into cars and trucks. Lightning flashed again and again, seeming to touch the trees around them. Violent, smashing thunder followed immediately.

Sue and Glory huddled together as wind and rain beat on the canvas roof of the convertible.

"They'll call it off now, won't they?" asked Sue.

"That's according to how long it stays like this," Glory told her. "In an ordinary rain they continue, but this is too much for even the most diehard horseman."

A few trucks and trailers left during the storm, but most stayed.

"I've had a grand time today, Glory," said Sue above the din.

"So have I. I couldn't have been any happier than I was when you won that prize. All of the hours of practice were worth it, weren't they?"

"Yes, but the practice was fun too," Sue told her. "It's fun working to improve yourself when you can feel the progress."

14.

For nearly twenty minutes they watched the storm sweep through the fairgrounds. At last there seemed to be less wind, and then less rain. When it slowed to not much more than a drizzle the loud-speaker blasted orders for the Grant Memorial Trail Horse Class to report to the west ring.

"Are you game to try, rain or shine?" asked Glory.

"Yes," Sue assured her. "If they have the class I want to be in it."

"That's the girl."

There wasn't any sense in trying to stay dry. The trees were dripping giant drops and a heavy drizzle was still falling. Within minutes the girls were soaked. Sue rode down to the ring and found only seven other contestants, a few of them in raincoats but most simply drenched in ordinary riding clothes stuck tight against wet skin.

Almost immediately, the ring began to be torn up by the horses' hooves, and soon it was a quagmire. Spray and hunks of mud flung up by the horse ahead spattered the riders. Sue found it was difficult to keep proper distance because it was so hard to see anything. At a canter she could feel Houri's hooves sinking into the mud and slipping on the turns.

Still, the ringmaster insisted on conducting the class completely, and that involved walk, trot, and canter in both directions. Dismounting to lead her mare over obstacles, Sue felt stiff as her wet riding pants stuck to her legs. Remounting, she discovered the saddle had become soaked in the few minutes she had not been sitting on it. Now the only part of her that had stayed dry became wet and uncomfortable.

She tried her best, but there was no excitement, no anticipation to this contest, only endurance. Since there were six ribbons and only eight entries, she was not surprised when she was given one, fourth place. She supposed that the judge, under his dirty hat, had been able to see more clearly than the contestants, because at least he had not been plastered with mud, as they had. Placing the ribbon on Houri's bridle, the judge smiled up at Sue and told her, "Be sure that both you and that chestnut mare of yours get a good rubdown now."

"She will, but I won't till I get home," Sue said.

"Spoken like a true horsewoman," he said as she rode out of the ring.

It was raining harder now, and she saw that Glory had turned the car and trailer around in preparation for leaving.

"Take a look in the car mirror," laughed Glory as Sue dismounted. She did, and found that her face was streaked where rivers of rain had run down through the spatters of mud.

They got Houri in the trailer, and both girls managed to squeeze in to give her a rubdown for fifteen minutes or so. Then they loaded the saddle and all other equipment into the Jaguar and got in. The tires made a squishy sound underneath them as they drove across the field to the road.

As they pulled out of the gate, another flash of lightning struck somewhere ahead of them and thunder followed it almost immediately. It began to pour again.

"Storm's circled around and come back," Glory observed.

The downpour was so severe that they could hardly see the road. She put on the headlights but that made little difference. The raindrops bursting on the pavement made a mist close to the road. Lightning flashed and the thunder could be heard in spite of the roar of rain on the canvas roof. Sue shuddered.

"You're cold," Glory said. "First diner we come to we'll get you a cup of hot chocolate."

"I'm all right," insisted Sue, her teeth chattering.

"You're cold, and you're tired, and you're in a state of shock after winning two ribbons in your first horse show," Glory said, shouting over the din of rain. "But it was all worth . . ."

A blue flash seemed to explode ahead of them. For a second they were blinded. The wind poured in torrents against the windshield. Wind lashed trees seen dimly along the side of the road. They heard above it all a tearing, snapping sound, and then Glory jammed on the brakes as a huge branch fell on the road in front of them. The car swerved from one side of the road to the other in a dizzy, sickening way.

Sue, helpless, could feel the movement, see the branch lying in their path. The Jaguar seemed to be drawn toward it, rushing to strike it. She heard the crunch of metal and glass, felt the car lift and turn. She was thrown against Glory, who fought to hold the wheel, then hurled against her own door. It gave, flew open, and she was in the air, flying through the rain. She landed on her hands and rolled over and over, then raised her head from the pavement.

Lightning flashed, and she saw the trailer tipped on its side, split open. There was a scream, the loudest, most chilling noise she had ever heard in her life, then a pounding and splintering of wood. A car was approaching and by its headlights she saw Houri rise from the wreck, stagger through the broken pieces.

The mare stood a second, then screamed once more and vanished into the rain. Sue tried to call but her voice didn't seem to carry against the roar of the wind in the trees and the downpour of rain on the road. It was like a silent yell in a nightmare where no one pays attention. She tried to stand up but one of her legs wouldn't work. She crawled, calling to the mare again and again, but Houri was gone.

Suddenly she thought of Glory, and then she lost consciousness.

She came to once. There were red flashing lights and blue flashing lights and men with flashlights. A policeman knelt down over her, shined a light in her eyes. He called to someone and she felt herself being lifted, the rain still pouring in her face. The pain in her leg shot through her body. She cried out, then fainted.

Again for a few seconds she regained consciousness. She felt that she was hurtling through the air once more. There was the scream of a siren and her bed jerked from side to side. She tried to raise up on her elbows, and said, "Where's Glory?"

She saw the blond hair in a bed near her, saw a bit of white face and bloodied bandages. She felt dizzy and fell back, hearing a buzzing in her ears, feeling blackness close in on her.

15.

The ceiling was made of squares of white. The walls were white and the bed and bedspread were white. A strange white bulge lay at the foot of her bed. It had toes sticking through a hole in it. She studied the room and the bed, then looked again at the thing with toes. She tried to move and felt a terrible pain. Then slowly she began to understand that the big white thing with the toes was her own leg in a plaster cast.

"I broke my leg," she said aloud. She felt sick, and

didn't know what to do. A nurse hurried into the room, took a quick look at her face, and held a basin for her.

She felt a little better afterwards, but the throbbing in her leg was steadily becoming stronger. She lay there enduring it, gritting her teeth, getting a handful of blanket and squeezing. The nurse returned.

"Where's Glory?" Sue's voice seemed hoarse, perhaps from screaming at Houri.

"She's under special care—concussion," the nurse told her.

"Is . . . is she in danger?"

"It's serious, but she seems to be making it okay. She broke her arm too. But they say that you're the lucky one."

"What do you mean?"

"Your side of the car was torn up. The Jaguar jumped over the branch after it hit, then threw you out and tipped on its side, where you would have been. The ambulance driver told me about it."

"Did they find Houri?"

The nurse looked puzzled. "Who's Houri?"

"My mare," answered Sue. "She was in the trailer."

"Oh, I thought it was a person," said the nurse. "I'm glad it was just a horse."

"It's not just a horse," Sue said, becoming tired suddenly. Tears began to fill her eyes. "She's a wonderful, wonderful chestnut mare, and she ran off after the crash, and she may be hurt."

"Okay. Okay," the nurse agreed. "The ambulance

driver figured that the trailer had been empty. Now wait, don't go to sleep, I've got to find out who you are. We got your friend's name off her license, but we couldn't find anything about you. We've got to inform your parents."

Drearily, half-awake, Sue tried to think how it would be possible to reach her dad, since they had no telephone. She heard another voice, the doctor's. She didn't open her eyes but fought to stay awake.

"Was she talking?" the doctor asked.

"Yes, I was just getting her to help us locate her parents."

"Never mind," he said. "Her name is Sue Servey and her father and uncle are on their way here now."

"How did you find them?" asked the nurse.

"Her brother drove up the highway on a motorcycle looking for the girls when they were late. He met the towtruck hauling the remains of the horsetrailer. Evidently he made a U turn, caught up to the towtruck, and got the driver to pull over to the side of the road and tell him about the accident. He was here earlier, while the girl was unconscious, then left to tell their father."

There was more conversation, but Sue passed beyond it into deep sleep.

Once again in the night she awoke, and cried out in pain. The nurse came and gave her a pill, and then she slept until morning.

By mid-morning she began to be awake for longer periods. The doctor examined her and then left. Shortly afterward the nurse washed Sue's face and brushed her hair. In a few minutes her father and Gore came in.

Somehow Bill in his overalls looked small as he hesitated at the doorway. He hurried toward her bed.

"Sue, are you all right except for the leg?" He bent over the bed and kissed her cheek.

"I guess so, Dad. My elbows and hands are all skinned up, and I've got some bruises, but they don't seem to be serious."

The nurse looked in and called cheerily, "Your friend Glory has come to now. It looks as if she's going to be all right."

"Thank God," said Bill.

"Amen to that," muttered Gore.

"First thing she did was to ask for you," the nurse said to Sue. "I told her that you were well enough to ask for her."

"Now there's only Houri to worry about," Sue said. "She ran away."

"Well, we'll look for her," Gore assured her. "She hadn't ought to be too hard to find, so don't worry."

Bones take a long time to knit, and there is no way to hurry them. For the first week there was Glory. The first time she was pushed into the room in a wheelchair Sue couldn't hold back a gasp, and then tears. It should have been enough that Glory was alive. But the sight of that beautiful face—scratched, bruised, swollen, and painted with antiseptic, her blond hair shaved around the bandage on her head was more than Sue could bear.

And then Glory tried to reassure her with a smile—a smile that was twisted because of swollen lip, and showed a missing front tooth.

"Cheer up, kid," she called. "I'd a lot rather be this way than in a coffin, although being dead would hurt a lot less, I'll bet."

That week went quickly, with Glory next door coming in frequently. The routine of the hospital was boring, but nurses' chores, doctor's visits, and meals broke up the day into fairly predictable pieces. The throbbing ache of the broken bone was always there, but pills kept it down so that sleep was possible.

When the old woman who shared the room with Sue moved out, Glory was wheeled in. "Might as well have your beds in the same room," said the nurse. "She's in here most of the time anyway."

Glory decided that it would be best if she flew home as soon as she was released. "My parents wanted to come here as soon as they heard about the accident," she told Sue. "But that would have been a big expense. I'm supposed to be quiet for six more weeks, and I'm sure they'll get enough of me in that length of time. I hate sitting around the house but I don't have much choice."

Bill and Gore spent all day that first Sunday looking for Houri. They cruised the roads in all directions, several miles back from the accident. They looked for tracks along dirt roads. They asked people at several farmhouses but no one had seen the chestnut mare. The men decided that either she had been hurt badly and died somewhere far from the road, or that someone had stolen her. They did not have the heart to tell either of the girls, however, and promised to go again the following Sunday. Bill placed an ad in the newspaper describing the mare and asking for information, but he received no answers.

Glory's face began to heal quickly. The swelling went down and some of the bruises and scratches disappeared. With her missing tooth, her one-sided haircut, and the bandage she was far from beautiful, but she looked cheerful when she left and was beginning to find her former store of energy.

"It's going to be tough trying to keep her quiet for another month," observed one of the nurses.

After Glory left, Sue felt a kind of sadness begin to flood over her. She couldn't stop thinking about the accident and all of the trouble it had caused—the injuries, the spoiling of Glory's lovely face, the loss of Houri, the demolished car. She spent hours thinking about it, going over and over the moments that had led up to the disaster. She thought that if she and Glory hadn't done this or that they would have been earlier and gone under the branch before it fell, or been later and seen the branch in the road in time to stop.

The worst thing was having to be in bed instead of going out to look for the mare. After Bill and Gore had spent the second Sunday searching at even greater distances from the scene of the crash, they told Sue that there couldn't be much chance of getting the mare back. They both believed that if she hadn't died of injuries she probably received in the crash, she must have been found along the road and stolen.

Sue could not let herself believe that Houri was really gone. She became impatient with everything and everyone. She wanted to stand up, but the doctor wouldn't let her. She wanted to go home but was told that she must remain in the hospital a little longer. Each refusal made her more depressed because each delayed the day when she could start off on her own search for her chestnut mare.

Her break was a bad one. The hospital would not let her go until another week had passed, three weeks in all from the accident. During those last two weeks Bill and Gore came evenings when they could, which wasn't often

Jack had taken a job in Philadelphia. He came to see her once, having driven hard all day Saturday and having to leave at noon Sunday. He had tried to get time off from his job in order to help in the search for Houri, but his boss had refused.

Janet and her father came to pick Sue up on the day she was to leave. The Lacys had a station wagon in which Sue could ride with her leg stretched out. Mr. Lacy had folded the back seat down and placed a mattress on the floor. "Just like an ambulance," he told Sue. Janet rode in the back with her for company.

At home time passed slowly. Janet visited as often as she could, but there was a lot of work for her at home. Everything in the vegetable garden seemed to be ready for harvest at once, and that meant helping with the freezing and canning. Gail, Fred's oldest daughter, visited every day. She washed Bill's breakfast dishes and packed him a lunch on workdays. And she did the sweeping and laundering and ironing—most of the things Sue did before the accident. In addition to being a willing worker, Gail was great company. She told stories of life in the city—of the poverty they had endured, of the rats in their wretched tenement, of the dangers of gang wars in the streets. Sue told her about school, especially about the teachers and about the boys and girls who would be in Gail's class. They became great friends during those weeks.

It was the end of August before Sue could begin to get around on crutches. By practicing on the steps leading to the door of the trailer, she learned how to get up and down well enough to climb on and off the school bus. The first days at school were difficult, because moving on crutches was different with people jostling and being impatient to get past. Teachers helped by letting her out of class early, and friends carried her books. Soon the crutches presented no problem, and she was able to get around almost as well as everyone else.

But the cast stayed on into late October. During that time she went out twice with Bill and Gore looking for Houri. Sue thought that some farmer might have found her and kept her in his pasture.

It was November before Sue could ride her bicycle, and even then long trips tired her leg and made it ache. She began to give up plans for bicycling on the back roads in a lone search for Houri. Winter came, and snow, making the roads impossible for bicycling. She would have to wait until spring. Never for a moment did she give up the idea that she would conduct her own search as soon as she could.

The winter hours were filled with homework and school projects and housework. Though she longed for the mare and for the companionship of Glory, she found herself drawn into busy routines that left little time to be sorry for herself. She found that Gail had taken her place as Janet's best friend, although sometimes the three of them talked for hours in the attic room. She was hurt by Janet's obvious preference for Gail as a friend. But Sue found herself tiring of their talk anyway. They seemed to dwell endlessly on trivial happenings and on details about the boys in their class at school, particularly the boys that were interested in girls.

It was only in the evening when she lay in bed awake, that a depressing loneliness came over her sometimes. She could hardly bear to think of the events between that Christmas morning when she threw her arms around the chestnut mare and the moment on the highway when she struggled to her hands and knees and saw by the lightning flash that the mare had freed herself from the splintered wreckage of the trailer. She tried to make herself have a good and happy dream about the mare but it never happened.

And so December, January, and February came and went. March brought more snow and set back her plans for searching. In early April the back roads were too muddy for bicycling. Sue became restless. It seemed as if everything had conspired to prevent her from finding her mare.

One day during April vacation a car drove into the yard. Sue got up to look out of the window, then yanked open the door and rushed out to throw her arms around Glory. She had missed the presence of the older girl many times during the winter, and they had written several times, but until that moment Sue had not realized the strength of their friendship. Now they just held on, overcome for the moment, letting the tears come in rivers.

Glory spoke in her ear a little gruffly, "You're still limping."

Sue suddenly remembered and pushed back to look into Glory's face. "You're beautiful again!" There was a trace of a scar just above her right eye, disappearing under her hair. That must be why she had changed the way she combed it. Sue didn't want to stare. She whispered, "Let me see how they fixed up the missing tooth."

"Just like new," Glory showed her. "You really couldn't tell which one was missing if you didn't already know."

"Do you two always cry when you see each other?"

Until that moment Sue hadn't noticed the man who had been in the car with Glory.

"Sue, this is Tom Staples. We work at the same

newspaper together and we're planning to go to graduate school next year."

Tom got out of the car and stretched out his hand to shake Sue's. He was quite tall with rather long curly hair and a moustache and a kind of impish smile. She liked his strong grasp on her hand.

"We're going to be a husband-and-wife lawyer team," he told her. "We won't argue, we'll debate."

"Right away?" Sue asked. "I mean, are you going to be married soon?" She realized immediately that it had been a tactless thing to ask and she felt her face getting red.

"We haven't decided when," Glory answered, and Tom added, "Only that it will be." They seemed so relaxed about it that Sue was no longer embarrassed by her blunt question.

Glory told her, "After six months of working for a newspaper we both decided that the only way to fight the kind of injustice we've been reporting is through the courts. So we are going back to college to get ourselves qualified to enter the battle."

"That's how we met," said Tom. "We kept finding ourselves on the same side of arguments. We were always against the same politicians and for the editor who was trying to expose them."

"And we still keep getting into trouble for reporting the news the way it really happened," said Glory shaking her head, "but that's a long story."

"Come on inside," Sue invited. "I'll make some coffee and we can sit down and talk."

As they stepped through the doorway, Glory said to Tom, "I'll bet you've never been in a mobilehome. See how big it is. There's more room in here than there is in a lot of houses, because it's so well planned."

"Show him around while I put on the coffee pot," offered Sue. "The beds are made and the floor is swept for once so I don't mind anybody looking."

As they began their inspection tour she called, "Maybe you'll get one when you're married, before you make your fortune."

When they came back into the living room Tom said, "I can't get over it. This thing looks so small from the outside, yet inside it has all the space you need. And everything is so handy."

Sue folded the dining room table down from the wall. "Try our multi-purpose living room."

As they sat down Glory became serious suddenly and said, "You never found Houri, did you? Did you ever hear anything about her?"

"No. Bill and Gore looked for two whole days, and they took me twice in the truck. They think that either she was hurt so bad that she died, or that someone stole her."

"What do you think?" asked Glory.

"I don't know, really. Sometimes I can still hear that scream she gave when the trailer tipped over. That makes me think that she must have been hurt really bad. But she ran away and kept going for long enough that we couldn't find her, so at least she must not have broken any bones. I haven't given up, you know. I've been waiting until I could ride my bicycle. I'm going to try all those back roads myself. I still think that someone somewhere may have found her wandering around and put her in a pasture."

"Why wouldn't they tell the people that run the horse show, or the Humane Society, or put an ad in the paper?" asked Tom.

Sue served the coffee and some cookies. "I figure that it could be somebody who would like to keep the mare if no one finds her. That means it would likely be someone on a back road far away from traffic—some road that we haven't found yet. I still think that there's a chance of it and I'm not giving up until I've tried them all. I'm going to bicycle all of those roads and ask at every house. Bill and Gore think that I'm crazy, but I'm not going to give up yet."

"Why don't we drive around for a while today?" asked Tom. "Maybe we can try some roads that you haven't gone on before."

"Won't a lot of those back roads be muddy now?" Glory asked.

"Some will be," said Sue. "Probably we shouldn't try it." She tried not to let her disappointment show.

"I say we should," said Tom, seeing. "If a road is too muddy we'll turn back. But most of them will be all right. After all, people live along them."

"It's nearly noon. Maybe I should make some

lunch before we leave," Sue suggested. "It's not much of a day for a picnic."

"We've got some things with us," Glory said, going out to the car. She brought in a bag of groceries from which they made toasted cheese sandwiches and soup.

Sue left a note for Bill and they piled into the front seat of the car, Sue between them.

They drove past the scene of their crash. Sue could never pass it without a shudder. "I had a feeling after the accident that Houri ran up that road," she said, "but we've been over it for about fifteen miles without finding anyone who saw her. We've been up and down the main road and on several side roads north and south of here. I don't know where to start over."

Tom felt that they should start with Sue's hunch. "Let's try all side roads branching from the road you think she took."

In the area of the crash, most roads branching from the main valley highway lead up from the flat farmland to steeper slopes with fewer open fields and many miles of forest. Some of the houses are small hunting camps, others are vacation homes for skiers or summer people. There are a few small farms.

Sue had never realized how many small gravel roads there were. Some connected with each other and many had other roads leading from them. It took a long time to follow each, stopping frequently to ask if anyone remembered seeing a loose horse go down the road one day last July.

"It seems strange asking people about something

that happened so long ago," Glory observed. "I sort of feel as if I have to explain the whole story, and that takes so long."

Tom thought that probably the storm that had caused the crash was also part of the reason that it was so hard to find the mare. "The noise of the wind and the rain, along with the thunder, may have been louder than the sound of the horse passing along a muddy road."

One farmer said that he remembered a single horse galloping by once last summer, but he had seen a friend of his leading one back home later. When they asked the friend he said that one of his horses had jumped a low section of fence and he had chased it down the road for miles before catching it.

At about three thirty in the afternoon they came to the end of another gravel road. There was a house there and a small barn, but no one was home.

"I've been up most of these roads before," Sue said, "including this one. I think that the house is only used by summer people. It always looks empty."

They turned around in the driveway and were just starting back down the road when they saw a car coming up toward them.

"There's no room to pass," Glory said. "We'll have to back up. If these are the people who live here we'll want to speak to them anyway."

The car drove into the yard. An elderly man and woman got out. Glory walked over to them and talked quietly for a minute. Then she motioned to Sue excitedly. "Come here and listen to this."

16.

"It was just about the end of July," the man told them. "I remember that there had been a terrible thunderstorm that afternoon—with a regular hurricane of a wind.

"Along about dusk we heard our stallion making a terrible racket. I got up and looked out of the window just in time to see him jump through a place in the fence that seemed to be broken. He must have just broken it, or maybe it broke when he jumped, or maybe the other horse broke it, but it had been . . ."

"Other horse?" Sue interrupted.

134

The lady, apparently the man's wife, said, "Yes. That's what caused the commotion. A mare—sort of chestnut colored—was standing out in the road, and of course that's what got the stallion excited."

"We rushed out," continued the man, "just in time to see the two of them racing up the road. They went around that sharp bend and then we couldn't see them any more."

"We heard them whinnying once and then they were gone," the woman added.

"Was the mare—did she seem hurt or anything?" asked Sue, almost unable to say the words.

"Well, I thought she looked a little lame in front," the man told them. "But Hattie didn't notice it. The horse certainly wasn't injured so seriously that it kept her from running off with the stallion. Was she yours?" he asked Glory.

"No, she was Sue's, and still is if we can find her."

"How come you're just looking now when you lost her last summer?" the man asked.

Glory told them briefly about the accident and their injuries. "Sue has never given up the hope of finding her mare," she finished.

"I'd invite you into the house for tea or coffee instead of having you stand out here in the driveway," said the woman named Hattie, "but we just arrived from New Jersey to spend a few days here. We haven't even opened up the house yet to air out after being closed all winter."

Glory introduced herself and Sue and Tom. The

couple were named Hutchins and they came to the farm every summer. Their daughter had lived with them each summer for several years and had raised thoroughbred horses. The stallion, named King Midas, was her most valuable stud. He had been a great jumper several years ago, and many of his offspring had been prizewinners.

"You did get him back after he ran away with Houri, didn't you?" Sue asked.

"Not that night," Mr. Hutchins told them.

"I went up that road for a couple of miles calling and rattling an oat bucket, but it was dark and I had to come back. We got up early in the morning, planning to make a search, and he was standing by the gate."

"Alone?" asked Sue.

"Yes," said Mrs. Hutchins. "We looked around to see if the mare had followed, but she hadn't."

"Where does this road go?" asked Tom.

"We're not sure," Mr. Hutchins said. "It really isn't passable by car beyond this point. I've walked about three miles along it. It goes up gradually for that distance and then starts down into another valley. There is a small town called Stratton over that way and people have told us this is the old stagecoach road that used to go there. This is supposed to come out at a place called Boles Hollow. I've often wanted to drive around and see if I could find the other end of it but I never got around to it."

"We'll let you know," Glory said, "because we're going to do that now."

Tom asked, "How far would you guess it is to where it becomes driveable again?"

The Hutchinses thought that it was about six miles through but at least thirty miles around by car.

"You see, I'm afraid that we won't know where we are when we get there by car," Tom said to Glory. "I think that it would be best if I hiked along this road while you two drive around. Then we can search for each other in Boles Hollow and when you find me we'll know where this road comes out."

"And we'll know where to start asking about Houri," said Sue.

"You've given us a lot of encouragement," Glory told them. "Sue never doubted that she would find her mare, but I must admit I wasn't so sure. Now I suddenly feel that we're on a trail."

"It's after four thirty," Mrs. Hutchins said to Tom. "Aren't you afraid that it will be dark before you hike to the other end of the road?"

"Not really," Tom laughed. "I've been on the track team at college, and I do a lot of long-distance running. This can be my exercise today."

Tom started up the road at a trot a few minutes later. Sue and Glory thanked the Hutchinses and got into the car. Mr. Hutchins called after them, "Let us hear from you. We'll want to know how it all comes out."

They drove in silence for a few minutes before Glory said, "Don't get your hopes too high. There's still a chance that she was stolen. The fact that she evidently wasn't injured badly makes her more valuable."

Sue sighed and then said, "I know. But this is sure a lot better than not having any idea if she was even alive."

They followed a road map to the town of Stratton. There were only a dozen houses and a shabby general store with a gas pump in front. Glory went into the store to ask directions, then came out and started up the car, saying, "They told me that if I take a left and then the second right I'll be on the Boles Hollow Road."

They found the turns, made them, and drove for about twenty minutes on a gravel road. At first the road climbed quite steeply, with wooded slopes rising on either side. Then it leveled and there was a narrow valley with several small dairy farms. Farther along there were fewer farms and some abandoned places with barns that looked ready to fall down.

The road came to an end abruptly at a small run-down farm. A huge dog, evidently part hound and part police dog, snarled savagely at them as they turned the car around in the driveway. An old man pushing a wheelbarrow loaded with stones came from behind the house. Glory lowered the window to speak to him, then closed it quickly when the dog put his front paws on the side of the car and started to put his head inside. She called her questions through a narrow opening.

The man stopped to listen but did not set down the wheelbarrow. He looked disapprovingly as Glory tried to explain their business. Then he said, "No, I didn't see a horse or a young man galloping by here, either today or last July," and walked away with his heavy load, shaking his head.

They backed the car out of the driveway. Glory laughed, "If I'd had a half-hour or so I think I could have made him understand why we were turning around in his driveway."

They drove slowly back along the gravel road.

"What can we do now?" Sue asked. "We reached the end of the road and Tom isn't here."

It was nearly dark and Glory was beginning to worry, but she said, "There are plenty of side roads we can try, and . . . wait! There's someone ahead walking along the road. I think it's Tom."

They honked the horn and he turned and saw them and waved.

When they reached him he got in beside Sue. "Back up until you get to that side road on the right. That's the one that the Hutchinses' road comes out on."

"Are there any places up there where we can ask about Houri?" Sue wanted to know.

"Yes, there are a couple of trailers and an old farm and a shack." They passed the trailers and a short distance farther a farm. The road went through about a half-mile of woods and then there was a small clearing. In the woods at the edge was a one-room shack. In the dusk it would not have been noticeable except for the faint light in the window.

"Stop here," said Tom.

A dog barked as he stepped from the car, but the

greeting turned into a friendly one as Tom patted a tail-wagging border collie. A light shown in the doorway of the shack and a woman was silhouetted on the threshold.

"Where's the girl that says she lost a chestnut mare?" she called.

"Here!" cried Sue. "If you know anything about her please tell me quickly. I've been trying to find her for such a long time!"

"Since about the thirtieth of last July?" asked the woman.

"Oh, yes!" said Sue. She discovered that she was shivering.

"Take this flashlight," said the woman. "At the far edge of the clearing—see where I'm shining the beam —is a stable with three horses in it. See if one of them belongs to you."

Sue took the flashlight and the woman warned, "Don't run, now. There's snags and rocks in the field and a fence at the far end."

Sue was off toward the stable, her lame leg slowing her hardly at all. Glory tried to follow, but without the light she couldn't keep up.

Sue heard a horse nicker. The sound was familiar. The flashlight needed new batteries and she could barely see by it. It was fading rapidly. Three heads looked out of the tops of their stall doors. The first head was large and black, the second reddish brown, the third—she looked back at the second. She stood on her tiptoes and beamed the dying flashlight into the stall. As she tried frantically to see by its thin glow the horse nickered again and nuzzled Sue's neck. Without seeing, Sue had no doubt then.

"Houri," she whispered and threw her arms around the mare's neck. She suddenly realized that she was sobbing, out of control, unable to do anything but cry and hang on.

Glory stumbled in the dark, muttering. "I can see a dark building, and I can smell horses, and I can hear you crying. All I can say is I hope it's a good cry and not a bad one."

Sue wasn't able to stop. She tried to say, "It's a good one," but wasn't sure that the words came out. She felt Glory's hand on her shoulder and then Glory was patting the mare and saying, "Well, Houri, you sly old fox, you sure did have us worried. I suppose you've been wondering why it took us so long to find you."

"I'll hold her while you open the door," she said to Sue. "You'd better look her over, that is, feel her over, since I don't think that flashlight will help much."

Sue went into the stall. She realized that she could not examine the mare thoroughly, but she had her pick up each foot to make sure there were none she could not stand on. She found some marks on her right shoulder but could not see clearly.

"She seems all right," said Sue, "except that she is terribly fat. I'd like to take her home right now."

"That may be a problem. Anyway let's find out what this lady has to say," suggested Glory.

They made their way back to the house. The flashlight was by now so weak that Sue had to look into it to see whether it was still on.

At the sound of their voices approaching, the woman opened the door of the shack and let them in. Sue was struck immediately by the taste and care with which the small building had been transformed into a very pleasant one-room home. The feature attraction was a wood-burning cook stove upon which was a loudly perking coffeepot. The room was comfortably warm and had a delicious wood-smoke-and-coffee smell. Various items of female clothing were hung unashamedly on wires stretched near the stovepipe.

Along one side of the room was a double-decker bunk, both beds made up. "That's my guest room," the lady said, noticing that Sue was looking at the upper bunk.

"Please tell me about Houri," Sue begged.

Tom said, "Now you all haven't been properly introduced. Mrs. Manroth and I met earlier this evening when I trotted out of the woods at the place where the Hutchinses' road becomes Mrs. Manroth's road. Mrs. Manroth, this is Sue Servey, the owner of the chestnut mare whose name, you now know, is Houri. And this is Glory Stein. Glory and I are going to be married in a few months."

With the completion of introductions came a few minutes of small talk during which it turned out that Mrs. Manroth had attended two years of Bickner College, "Before you were born," she told Glory. It also was revealed that Mrs. Manroth raised prize milking goats which she kept in a small shed behind her shack.

"Call me Josie," she told them. "While you were out in the stable Tom told me how you lost your mare. That's a much more exciting story than how I found her, because all I did was walk out one morning and there she was. My two, one a gelding and one a mare, were still shut in the stable. Your mare was grazing just outside of the fence. I walked up to her and she stood right there while I petted her.

"Then I noticed that her right shoulder was all cut up. I didn't think of her being in an automobile accident. I just figured that she must have got tangled up with a fence. The cuts were bad enough to make her limp. You'll see the scars tomorrow; the hair that came back in around them is white."

Sue started to ask a question but Josie, noticing, answered it. "No, she doesn't limp any more. That only lasted for a few days.

"I put antiseptic and a salve on the cuts. Then I decided that she might get into more trouble running around the country loose, so I put her in the goat pasture for the rest of the day. When nobody came looking for her that day I put her in the barn at night. Nobody came the next day either, so I went down the road and asked if anyone knew about a stray horse, and no one did.

"I figured she might have come through the woods road, but nobody came after her and I didn't know where the road went, so I stopped worrying about it. After a week or so I tried a saddle on her and found that she was well trained and that she could jump."

"Glory helped me train her," Sue explained.

"Houri had just placed very well in the Arlingham Horse Show the day we had the accident," Glory added.

Josie continued, "I told people at the general store at Stratton. And I watched for ads in the newspaper."

"We put one in for a week," Sue told her.

"What paper?"

"The *Valley Transcript*," said Sue.

Tom said, "I'll bet you don't get that here."

"No, we don't," said Josie. "Actually I don't get any newspaper, but for two weeks I subscribed to the one everyone around here buys, which is the *Chester Herald.*"

"No wonder you didn't see our ad," Sue said, and then suddenly realized that this wasn't a very profound observation.

"At any rate," Josie continued, "I kept the mare over the fall and winter and now into spring. I had begun to think of her as mine because it seemed as if no one would ever come after her."

For the first time, it occurred to Sue that she had some problems to worry about. She asked the first question of Glory. "How will I ever get her home? It must be seventy miles the way we came. And we don't have a trailer any more."

Glory had already thought of the second problem that was bothering Sue. "You've been feeding grain and hay to the mare for almost nine months. How much do you figure she cost you?"

"I think I can solve both of your problems at once," said Josie, "if you are willing to make a trade."

"What kind of a trade?" asked Sue, who suddenly had the chilling thought that Josie was going to try to keep the chestnut mare in return for one of her own horses. "I don't have anything to trade, and I certainly don't want any horse but Houri."

Josie said, "I've been waiting to see if you knew about this or if it happened when your mare ran off with the stallion. Here is my proposition. Let me keep Houri the rest of this spring, until school is out. She shouldn't be moved now anyway, and I'll tell you why in a minute.

"Then I'll transport her to your place. I can get a trailer when I need one. I have a friend who lets me borrow it. And I won't charge you anything for her board for the months she's been here. In return . . ."

"Yes, what in return?" asked Sue.

"In return you let me keep her foal."

"Her foal! *That's* why she seemed so fat," Sue cried.

"By the Hutchinses' stallion, old what's-his-name!" said Glory.

"King Midas, winner of countless blue ribbons and sire of high jumpers," Tom reported.

"Wow," said Glory. "That's kind of a bargain."

Sue thought a minute and then said, "I think that it's fair. Houri has been fed and taken care of all fall and winter. She's been eating hay and grain at Josie's expense. She shouldn't be moved right now anyway. And I don't have a horse trailer. We'd probably have to pay thirty dollars or more to get her transported, and Bill doesn't have that kind of money to spare. He's still paying hospital and doctors' bills."

"Is a foal worth a lot of money?" asked Tom.

"Not until after you've fed it for about three years and spent a lot of time training it," said Josie. "And even then there's the risk that the animal will be deformed or mean or sickly."

"I think it's fair," said Sue for the second time.

"And any time you can get a ride over here, you're welcome," Josie told her. "You can stay for a weekend or a week. I don't serve any fancy foods here. I don't even have a refrigerator because I don't have electricity. But I make out all right and I guess you will too."

"I'd love to come," said Sue. "Is it all right if I try to get Bill to bring me next weekend?"

"The sooner the better," Josie assured her. "There won't be anyone here but me. I've got a grandson a little younger than you who visits me for a couple of weeks during the summer, but that's all. Of course you won't be able to ride Houri until a while after she has the foal, but you can ride either of mine. I've even got two saddles so that we can ride together."

"Oh great!" said Sue. "Maybe we could follow this road back to see Mr. and Mrs. Hutchins and I could tell them about finding Houri."

"Fine," agreed Josie. "I've been to the top of the

hill but not down the other side and I've always wanted to."

She had been busy at the stove while she talked. Now she said, "You folks have been so busy worrying about that horse I'll bet you haven't eaten. Well, I live alone and I don't have much in the house, but you'll have to eat a plate of beans before you go." She ladled out plates of steaming baked beans and told them, "You'll have to hold your plates in your hands, because I don't have a table big enough for four."

She sliced bread, buttered it, and handed it around. She passed a small jar with a butter knife in it to Sue. "Try some of my honey. I keep bees here, too. I put up about eight gallons a year and use it most of the time instead of sugar. I don't treat it or heat it or do anything else to it and it turns thick and white, perfect for spreading on bread."

She pointed to the jars on shelves along the wall. "I pick berries by the gallon—blackberries, blueberries, black raspberries, anything that is good to eat. And I put them up in jellies and preserves for the winter."

"Who cuts your firewood?" asked Tom.

"I do myself, and I have for years. I've never had a husband while I lived in this place. You see, the first husband and I never got along. The second one was killed in the Second World War. The third marriage was worse than the first. After we parted I decided I wasn't doing very well and that I shouldn't marry any more. Now I live here and enjoy it. I seem to be able to get

147

along with the animals. I never have much money but I don't need much. Most of my spending is on the animals. But don't worry," she said to Sue. "I'm not as bad to live with as I used to be. And it's especially easy to live with me if you don't mind animals," she added with a grin.

"Oh, I'll come all right if I can get here," Sue told her.

"Don't try to phone, because I don't have a telephone," Josie said. "Just come. I'll always be ready."

There were a few moments of silence, broken only by the sound of forks scraping the last trace of baked beans off empty plates.

"Poor Bill will be worried about you," Glory said to Sue. "We'd better get going right away."

"Oh, that's right." Sue suddenly realized that it was quite late and that they had a long drive before they would be home.

They thanked Josie and she stepped outside in the dark with them as they got into the car.

"I'll be back as soon as Bill can get me here, this coming weekend I hope," Sue called as they drove away.

"I still think that was sort of a hard bargain to make with a kid your age," Glory said.

"No," said Sue. "You only think it's hard because it's fair. She didn't give me a big break because of my age. She treated me like she would anyone else, I'll bet, and that's all right with me. It's just as Bill says, 'You can't just take all the time. You've got to give a little.' "

"You be careful you don't grow up too fast," Tom told her.

148

Sue leaned back and closed her eyes. "I feel that learning to ride and going to the horse show and getting into the accident were all a part of my life, like a chapter in a book," said Sue. "But nothing seemed right and the chapter couldn't come to an end until I found out what happened to Houri. I couldn't love an animal that much and just forget about her. Now that I know she's all right and that I'm going to get her back it all fits into place and I feel good again. I know that I'm going to do a lot more riding, and Bill promised to make me a horse trailer so that I can get to a horse show once in a while. But it seems to me that just about as soon as one thing is completed something else begins, and I'm kind of always looking for the next thing. That's the feeling I have right now, that something is completed, and it is really a good feeling."

Tom looked across Sue to Glory on the other side of the car. "I wish I had her secret for getting so much out of life."

Glory shook her head. "At twenty-two you and I are too old."

ABOUT THE AUTHOR

PHILLIP VIERECK was born in New Bedford, Massachusetts. He attended Dartmouth College (B.A.) and Plymouth College (M.Ed.). Since 1948 he has held various teaching positions in Alaska and Vermont.

Mr. Viereck is Supervisor of Elementary Education in Bennington, Vermont, and says that he did a bit of construction, fishing, and truck driving in his "younger days."

He and his wife, Ellen, who is a junior primary teacher, have collaborated on five books for young people, *Independence Must Be Won, Eskimo Island, Let Me Tell You About My Dad, The Summer I Was Lost,* which won the Thomas A. Edison Award for 1965 for Special Excellence in Contributing toward the Character Development of Children, the Dorothy Canfield Fisher Children's Book Award for 1967, and a Lewis Carroll Shelf Award for 1970; and *The New Land,* which was awarded a Citation of Honor from the Society of Colonial Wars.

The Auerecks and their four children live in a colonial farmhouse (which they restored) in North Bennington, Vermont.